"Isabel, I want you to meet somebody."

Eli was standing in the doorway looking at her.

"Okay." She smiled and tried to see around him. Maybe he had a new partner, although why he'd have Isabel come all the way over here for that–

"Come here, Susie-Q," Eli said, reaching behind his back. He tugged a small child into view by the hand– a little girl so beautiful it made Isabel's eyes sting. She looked at Eli for an explanation.

"She's deaf and doesn't speak, Isabel, but she showed up at the orphanage yesterday with nothing but the clothes on her back and one shoe. And this."

He lifted his other hand to show her a sealed plastic bag containing a closed switchblade knife.

THE TEXAS GATEKEEPERS:
Protecting the borders...and the women they love.

Books by Elizabeth White

Love Inspired Suspense

Under Cover of Darkness #2
Sounds of Silence #11

*The Texas Gatekeepers

ELIZABETH WHITE

As a teenager growing up in north Mississippi, Elizabeth White often relieved the tedium of history and science classes by losing herself in a romance novel hidden behind a textbook. Inevitably she began to write stories of her own. Torn between her two loves—music and literature—she chose to pursue a career as a piano and voice teacher.

Along the way Beth married her own Prince Charming and followed him through seminary into church ministry. During a season of staying home with two babies, she rediscovered her love for writing romantic stories with a Christian worldview. A previously unmined streak of God-given determination carried her through the process of learning how to turn funny mushy stuff into a publishable novel. Her first novella saw print in the banner year 2000.

Beth now lives on the Alabama Gulf Coast with her husband, two high-maintenance teenagers and a Boston terrier named Angel. She plays flute and pennywhistle in a church orchestra, teaches second-grade Sunday school, paints portraits in chalk pastel and—of course—reads everything she can get her hands on. Creating stories of faith, where two people fall in love with each other and Jesus, is her passion and source of personal spiritual growth. She is always thrilled to hear from readers c/o Steeple Hill Books, 233 Broadway, Suite 1001, New York, NY 10279, or visit her on the Web at www.elizabethwhite.net.

Sounds *of* Silence

ELIZABETH WHITE

Steeple
Hill®

Published by Steeple Hill Books™

STEEPLE HILL BOOKS

Steeple Hill®

ISBN 0-373-44227-0

SOUNDS OF SILENCE

Copyright © 2005 by Elizabeth White

www.SteepleHill.com

Printed in U.S.A.

The Lord protects the foreigners among us.
He cares for the orphans and widows, but
He frustrates the plans of the wicked.
—*Psalms* 146:9

This book is dedicated to the missions ministry of First Baptist North Mobile. Keep on serving and sharing the Good News!

I'm grateful for my critique partners—Scott, Tammy and Sheri—and my editor, Diane Dietz. You make me a better writer.

Thanks as well to several people who lent their expertise as I researched details for this book. Glenda Perkins, teacher of hearing impaired students in Mobile County Public Schools, read the manuscript and gave great suggestions. ATF agent and former Border Patrol Agent Michael Knoll answered about a million questions with great patience and clarity. Cena Goff helped with nursing issues, and Ken Foster—firefighter extraordinaire—answered questions regarding, well, fires. Susan Howell answered a couple of horse questions. All mistakes are mine.

My friend and fellow author Jane Myers Perrine helped once more with Spanish translation. Thanks for your time, *señora*.

I would never have been able to give this book the richness of detail it deserved, without observing and interviewing several of God's choice servants who minister on the Texas/Mexico border. Rosie, Aurora, Pastor Pablo, Dennis, Terry and others involved with Texas River Ministries—I pray for you regularly. Thank you for letting me share Christ in your corner of the world.

Prologue

Ciudad Acuña, Mexico

Mercedes woke up when something nudged her in the ribs. By the reddish light coming through the beaded curtain, she could see her sister Lupe's slender feet in scarlet high-heeled sandals. She sat up, rubbing her eyes and yawning.

Lupe had on a black leather miniskirt and a white blouse that glowed like neon in the dark storeroom. She'd let Mercedes try on the skirt yesterday, but it had reached to her knees. Laughing and showing all her beautiful white teeth, Lupe had clipped the waistband with a clothespin so that Mercedes could walk in it without tripping.

One day she would be beautiful, too, and men would buy her presents like the earrings that dangled against Lupe's neck.

But not Pablo. She'd stay away from that bad *hombre*. He was handsome, with slick black hair and nice teeth, but he was mean. He gave Lupe a white powder that made her silly. Pablo had also given Lupe the black scab that cut across one of her fine eyebrows, and the bruises on her back.

Mercedes gasped when Lupe reached down and yanked her to her feet. She could tell Lupe was upset, moving her red lips in patterns too sloppy to follow, without trying to sign with her hands. Repeating herself, she shook Mercedes so hard her head snapped back.

No! Mercedes signed, jerking out of Lupe's hands. *That hurts.*

Lupe's kittenish face crumpled, tears streaking her makeup and leaving black mascara tracks under her eyes.

Get out, Lupe signed. *Danger.*

Mercedes shook her head. *I don't want to—*

Lupe suddenly shoved Mercedes to the floor and glanced at the doorway. The beads swung as something bumped against them. Lupe's face wrinkled in panic, and her lips moved—"Run!"

She turned to peer through the curtain.

Mercedes was pretty scared, but curiosity won over fear. Better to keep an eye on things than to run away like one of the chickens behind Hector's bar. She crept toward Lupe on her hands and knees, feeling odd, thumping vibrations through the tile floor.

Kneeling beside her sister, Mercedes blinked against the sudden light of the neon signs above the bar. As her eyes adjusted, she scanned the scene. In the center of the room, surrounded by empty tables—it must be close to daybreak if there were no customers—two men were fighting. One was Pablo, dressed in tight black trousers and a black silk shirt. A sneer curved one side of his handsome mouth. He had both fists knotted at the throat of a tall, skinny *Americano* man whom Mercedes had seen a couple of times. She didn't know the white man's name, but figured he was rich. He gave Lupe money for soft drinks and cigarettes, and he'd bought her the black leather skirt.

Mercedes sucked in a gasp. The *gringo* was about to stick a pearl-handled switchblade into Pablo's gut.

Then the fight quickly ended when Pablo reached down and yanked the knife from the other man. Twisting it, he thrust upward. The *gringo* sagged as Pablo stepped away.

Lupe grabbed Mercedes, who watched in horror as Pablo calmly wiped the knife clean and folded it shut. But as he stooped to lift the victim's body under the arms, the knife slipped out of his hand and fell to the floor. Cursing, Pablo dragged the body outside, leaving the door open.

Shuddering as if she might fall apart, Lupe pulled Mercedes to her feet. *Run! Danger!* Lupe signed. *Through the hole. I'll be right there.* She tried to shove Mercedes toward the back wall of the tiny room.

Mercedes started to obey, but when Lupe darted into the empty barroom, she followed. She watched through the beads as her sister snatched up the knife with the tail of her blouse. Nearly mowing Mercedes down on the way back, Lupe grabbed her by the arm and shook her roughly. *Go through the hole!* she signed. *Hurry!*

Frightened by the knife still clutched in Lupe's other hand, Mercedes started to cry. *Come with me,* she signed. *I'm scared.*

Lupe calmed a bit, and Mercedes could see she was thinking hard. Getting down on her hands and knees, Lupe reached under the cot and found a plastic grocery sack. She dropped the knife in it and knotted the handles. *I'm right behind you,* she signed. *Go!*

Mercedes nodded. Maybe it would be all right.

Taking a deep breath, she scrambled under the bench against the wall, which was made out of a splintery two-by-four and a couple of cinder blocks. Behind the bench was a loose flap in the tar paper wall, which she used in the middle of the night when she needed to visit the outhouse.

She was about to go through the flap, when she felt heavy thumping footsteps against the floor. *Pablo.* He was coming. Peeking from under the bench, she saw his expensive shoes and Lupe's red sandals. They were grappling hard, almost like a crazy kind of dance.

Mercedes's heart jumped when the bag holding the knife fell to the floor right in front of her face. Without stopping to think she grabbed it and pulled it toward her. Obviously Lupe didn't want Pablo to have it.

She should leave now. But what about Lupe? Was there anything she could do to help her sister? Flattening herself against the floor, she looked up and saw Lupe's trembling knees, the flashing jewels in her ears.

And Pablo's evil face, contorted in rage. He had Lupe by the neck, choking her.

A wrenching silent scream tore her throat muscles.

Pablo flung Lupe to the floor just as Mercedes dove for the opening in the wall. She wriggled through head first, and had made it out to the waist before she felt Pablo toss the board aside.

She crawled madly, gashed her knee on a loose nail, and the pain stopped her.

Mistake. Pablo grabbed her heel.

She jerked her foot out of his fingers, pulling off her shoe, and shoved her hands hard against the wall. She burst into the open night air, tumbled down the rocky hill, and sat up when she reached the bottom.

Bruised and panting, she scrambled to her feet clutching the bag with the knife in it. Pablo would come after her, but it was a moonless night, and she knew the alleys of the colony better than he did. She had hidden herself many times when necessary.

She knew a place to hide that he'd never think of.

Mercedes took off running toward the hill where the Americans had built that big tin building last summer. She dodged from building to building, zigzagging so that Pablo couldn't follow her.

Looking up, she saw the cross on the church at the top of the hill. Funny that it glowed so brightly, as if it were lit from within. No other light anywhere. The shape of the cross eased her fear.

She'd be safe when she got there.

Chapter One

Eli Carmichael was doing the Chicken Dance in a Mexican orphanage when God got his attention.

Encircled by children, he spun around with little Dulce Garcia clinging to his back. Despite two noisy floor fans, sweat was dripping off his nose and his T-shirt stuck to his chest. It was about 10:00 a.m. on this *Cinco de Mayo* morning, and impressive drafts of sunshine poured through the open windows onto the concrete floor. Had to be around a hundred and twelve degrees in here.

Even courting heat exhaustion, Eli knew what he'd seen: a mop of long black hair and two big dark eyes peeking around the doorway of the half wall between the dining hall and the chapel. As an experienced Border Patrol agent, he was used to noticing details. Furtive movements. Odd sounds and smells.

Eli blinked when he came around again. The little girl had disappeared.

The children dissolved in giggles as Dulce pointed over Eli's shoulder at his younger brother Owen, who was in the kitchen flirting with the pretty young housemother, Bernadette Malone, better known as Benny.

"O-wen! O-wen! O-wen!" the children chanted, clapping and stomping in unison. Eli grinned, set Dulce down and headed toward the kitchen.

"You've got to be kidding." But Owen goodnaturedly allowed himself to be dragged into the game. As the children held hands and skipped, Eli watched his brother execute a barely recognizable Macarena.

"Who's that little girl hiding back in the chapel?" Reaching around Benny, who was drying dishes in front of the sink, he snagged a bottle of water out of the refrigerator.

"What little girl?"

"About this high." Eli measured at his waist. "Long black hair and big brown eyes."

Benny gave him an amused look. "You just described every girl in the room."

"I didn't get a good look at her. She ducked when she caught me looking at her."

Benny turned to count the children. "Ten," she finished aloud. "They're all right there, Eli."

"I guess I was mistaken." But he knew he wasn't. Something fearful in those eyes made him ease back into the dining hall.

Skirting his brother and the circle of children, Eli slipped down the side of the Quonsetlike building. He ducked below the chest-high partition, beyond which rows of old-fashioned wooden theater seats faced a homemade lectern.

There was not much to steal here at *Los Niños de Cristos* Orphanage, but Eli didn't like the fact that Benny and the children were vulnerable to intruders. Like many areas along the border, the crowded colony around the orphanage lacked sanitation, clean water and law enforcement. It was full of unsupervised children whose parents worked in the American-owned factories on the outskirts of the city. Teenaged boys ran in packs, stealing anything that wasn't tied down.

The children's singing and the roar of the fans covered any noise his sneakers might have made as he approached. At the doorway of the partition, Eli quickly stepped around the wall.

She cowered under the folding table against the wall, both hands covering her face, knees drawn up under her chin. Honey-colored forearms were mottled with bruises, one knee gashed open. Dried blood ran down that leg into a blue flowered tennis shoe. The other foot was bare, the toes scraped and the sole black with dirt.

He'd seen it a hundred times and never got used to it. Eli shut his eyes to get himself together before he acted.

Lord, give me Your strength and wisdom. This little one's Yours. Help me not to scare her.

He got down on one knee. Except for a rhythmic shuddering, she didn't move. He waited, taking in more details. She wore a pair of baggy purple gym shorts with a pink halter top. A string of multicolored plastic beads encircled one skinny wrist. Her fingers were delicate, perfectly formed. She was small, about the size of Eli's five-year-old neighbor, Danilo Valenzuela.

The boy's mother, Isabel, would melt if she saw this one.

After a moment of watching the little girl, his heart splintering into painful shards, Eli reached out a cautious hand. Ready to grab her when she bolted, he touched her bare foot.

As expected, the hands came down, but the expression on that flowerlike face struck him like a fist in the stomach. The eyes were fearless, narrowed in challenge, leaving Eli measured and found wanting. The tender mouth squared to reveal a set of clenched white baby teeth, missing the two upper front ones.

Which told him she was around seven years old.

He had no idea what he expected her to do, but it certainly wasn't to reach behind her and flick open a pearl-handled switchblade knife.

Eli froze.

"Hey, sweetie, I'm Eli," he said hoarsely in Spanish. "I'm not gonna hurt you. What's your name?"

She continued to stare at him with fierce concentration, right in the eyes.

He smiled and dropped his gaze to the knife. There was dried blood on it. "Where'd you get that, baby? You need to give it to me before you cut yourself."

Her knuckles whitened. He could hear her breath hissing between her teeth.

"Is that how you hurt your knee?" He turned his hand palm-up. "Come on…"

The knife shook in her fist. Eli looked up to find dark eyes, the color of sunflower centers, focused on his mouth. Her lips began to tremble.

"Thank You, Jesus," Eli whispered when he felt the heavy coolness of the knife handle in his palm. "What's your name?" he asked again.

She shrugged and knuckled her eyes.

Helpless, he looked around. If he went to get Benny, his little housebreaker might vanish. Absently he closed the knife and stuck it in the pocket of his jeans. He was on his own.

"We're playing a game over there." He tipped his head in the direction of the children's laughter. "Wanna play?"

Big Eyes shook her head. But she leaned toward Eli.

"Okay, then we'll just watch." He extended his hand again, curling the fingers upward. "Come on."

There was a long pause. To Eli's relief, she laid her dirty little hand in his and let him help her out from under the table. She craned her neck looking up at him, and he smiled, but her expression remained serious.

Now what?

Isabel Valenzuela knew trouble when she saw it coming.

It had knocked on her door with alarming regularity since the day her son made his noisy entrance into the world. Five trips to the Del Rio Hospital ER and a standing appointment with the kindergarten teacher at Bethany Christian school had left her with no illusions about her parenting skills.

And when Eli Carmichael walked around the side of her house in full Border Patrol uniform at ten o'clock on a Monday morning, she knew she was in for it.

Mean Green. Big Trouble.

"Hey, Isabel, where's Danilo?" Eli braced both hands on the endpost of the clothesline as if he had all day.

"He's in school." She continued to peg tiny spider-web-design briefs on the line. "What's he done now?"

Eli gave her one of his slow grins, and Isabel suddenly wished she'd done more than twist her hair into a knot and stick a pencil in it this morning. Which was ridiculous. This was just Eli.

"He hasn't done anything," Eli said. "That I know of. I just need you to come with me to the station." When Isabel's eyes widened, he added hastily, "I need a favor. Nothing to do with Danilo."

She frowned. As one of her late husband's colleagues, Eli had for over a year taken it upon himself to help her and Danilo whenever they needed a man's hand. He lived in an apartment down the street, and he was single, unattached and apparently lonely. So she'd humored him, letting him mow her grass and take Danilo fishing. Occasionally she baked him a plate of brownies in return.

That was it. Had he suddenly decided to change the game plan?

"Come with you to the station," she repeated, stalling. "I'm pretty busy." She kicked a bare foot at the wicker basket full of clothes.

"I'll help." Before Isabel could protest, he'd grabbed

a couple of clothespins out of the cloth bag hanging on the line and reached into the basket.

Isabel worked beside Eli in silence for a full minute before she couldn't stand it any longer. "So what do you need me at the station for?" She hadn't been there since a week after Rico died, when she'd gone to pick up the stuff from his desk and locker.

Eli stopped whistling and looked at her over the top of a pale blue sheet. It was just about the color of his eyes. "I'm gonna let you take a look for yourself." He leaned in to sniff the sheet. "This smell reminds me of my grandma's house. She always let me hang clothes with her."

"Bleach," Isabel said. "I wondered why a single man would be so good at this."

"See, you never know about people," he said obscurely. "You had any bites on the house lately?"

He was talking about the For Sale sign in her front yard. Isabel beamed at him. "The agent called this morning. She's bringing a couple by this afternoon. Sounds promising."

Eli pursed his lips. "Oh."

"I really need to sell," Isabel reminded him. "I want to get settled in San Antonio before Danilo starts first grade. Wouldn't be good to move him in the middle of the school year."

"Yeah, I know." He still didn't sound particularly happy. "Maybe you should consider staying here."

"Eli, we've been over this. My parents are dying to have us back in San'tone. Danilo's their only grandson.

Besides—" she pinned a washcloth with vicious energy "—the memories in this house are getting to me. Everywhere I look I see..." She hid behind the sheet, embarrassed to inflict such personal angst on a guy who was, after all, just a neighbor. It had been a year and a half since Rico died. Time to move on.

To her astonishment, Eli pushed the sheet aside and ducked under the line. He stood less than a foot away, tall and masculine in that crisp green uniform that reminded her so achingly of Rico. Then Eli took off his hat, revealing curly, sun-streaked hair and those sky-colored eyes. Isabel looked away.

This man wasn't at all like Rico. Rico had been the life of any party, talking and joking and introducing anything that breathed to his Lord and Savior Jesus Christ. Eli, she knew, was only thirty or so, but seemed older. Quiet, almost taciturn. She got the feeling he was afraid of her, which in turn made her very uncomfortable.

"Isabel," he said. She looked up at him and flinched at the sorrow in those piercing eyes. "I'd bring him back if I could."

"I know you would." She lifted her shoulders. "But he's gone, and Danilo needs his grandpa. I've just got to get away from here."

He sighed. "I guess I can understand that." He set his hat back on his head. "Are you ready to go now?"

"Soon as I find my shoes and lock up the house."

Isabel set the empty basket against her hip and picked her way through the backyard, skirting Danilo's sand pile, which was littered with dump trucks, plastic buckets and bent spoons confiscated from her kitchen.

As she entered the small laundry room off the kitchen, she fretted anew at the sad state of the screen door and back step. She'd bought paint with last week's alterations money, but it was going to be a while before she had time to deal with it. Five bridesmaid dresses, all to be fitted and hemmed by next Friday, hung in her spare bedroom closet. Plus there was the puppet stage curtain she'd agreed to make for Bible School.

Painting and rescreening a door, as important as it was, would have to wait. Maybe the people who came this afternoon wouldn't look too closely.

Isabel left Eli fiddling with the back door light fixture—which Danilo had somehow broken with the baseball bat his grandpa gave him for his birthday—and went in search of her flowered flip-flops. If she had to *be* a matronly widow, at least she didn't have to *look* like one. On the way past her bedroom mirror, she remembered the pencil in her hair.

Good grief. Quickly she loosened the shoulder-length black mass and ran a brush through it. Lipstick? Sure, why not. Pink to match her shoes. She grimaced at her plain white blouse and denim capris, but decided not to change. Pathetic when a trip to the local Border Patrol station became a social outing.

Wondering why in the world Eli needed her there, she nearly ran head-on into him as she reentered the kitchen.

"Oops." He steadied her with big warm hands on her

shoulders. "I came in to test the light switch, and thought I'd check your fire alarm battery while I was in here."

Isabel caught her breath. He'd never been inside her house before. She was careful about appearances. "Thank you," she murmured. "I'm ready, so we'd better go. I have to pick up Danilo at noon."

"Okay." He quickly let her shoulders go, then turned to open the kitchen door for her. "You need a new battery, by the way."

Isabel pulled herself together as she entered the Border Patrol station. For some reason, it helped to stay close to Eli. He put a hand on her elbow as if sensing her discomfort, held the door for her and seated her in his office.

The Border Patrol community had been her family since the day Rico had moved her to Del Rio as an eighteen-year-old bride. She'd met her husband when she was a junior in high school and Rico a sophomore at UT San Antonio. Her parents had begged her to finish her own education, but because Rico could talk the paint off the walls—a trait their son shared—they'd eventually caved in and given their blessing to the wedding.

And, oh, how happy she and Rico had been! Isabel had quickly adjusted to the desertlike climate and learned to laugh at the idea of landscaping with cactus, mesquite and rocks. They'd found a little evangelical church that suited both their backgrounds and gave Rico an outlet for his love of music. Rico's partner, Jack Torres, had been a tough nut to crack, but eventually even he couldn't resist Rico's insouciant conviction that Christ was the answer to every need. Jack became a believer and literally spent most waking moments in Isabel's living room, learning to be a disciple.

Now, watching Eli disappear into the dispatch room, Isabel twisted her wedding rings and tried to remember those good times. It wasn't healthy to dwell on the tragedy that had mown her down like a freight train.

The train had also run over Eli, whose father had been the one responsible for the events that affected all their lives. But he didn't let it send him into depression. From what she could tell, Eli plowed right on, never looking back. Isabel often wondered what it would take to shake him up.

"Isabel, I want you to meet somebody." Eli was standing in the doorway looking at her.

She jumped, afraid in a crazy sort of way that he'd been reading her thoughts. How silly. "Okay." She smiled and tried to see around him. Maybe he had a new partner, although why he'd have Isabel come all the way over here for that—

"Come here, Susie-Q," Eli said, reaching behind his back. He tugged a small child into view and held her by the hand—a little girl with long, black braids and big, dark brown eyes, appearing to be about six or seven. Hispanic, judging by the golden-brown skin, and so beautiful it made Isabel's eyes sting.

Isabel looked at Eli for explanation.

He cleared his throat. "She's deaf and doesn't speak, Isabel. We can't get her to tell us her name or where she came from or anything. She showed up at the orphanage yesterday with nothing but the clothes on her back and one shoe. And this." He lifted his other hand to show her a sealed plastic bag containing a closed switchblade knife.

Isabel took a sharp breath. "Benny didn't know her?"

Eli shook his head. "Owen and I took some food over there for *Cinco de Mayo,* and stayed to play for a bit." He smiled down at the little girl, who was staring at her feet. Apparently somebody had given her a pair of sandals. They were too big, and had rubbed a blister on one foot. Eli jiggled her hand until she looked up at him with sober trust. "When I caught her hanging around, she like to've spitted me with the knife. Didn't you, Little Bit?"

Isabel watched the little girl's lips curl upward ever so slightly. She seemed to understand she was being teased. There was extreme intelligence behind those dark chocolate eyes. "So what's she doing here? She's Mexican, I presume."

"Kind of a convoluted story." Eli leaned against the door frame. "I left her there with Benny, but I took the knife. This morning, Bryan Hatcher's body was found on the riverbank."

Isabel gasped. "Pam and Rand's son?" Pam was a member of their church, her husband a well-to-do rancher with friends in the state legislature. Both were well-respected in the community.

"Yep." Eli showed Isabel the knife's beautiful pearl handle. It had a raised gold initial "H" near one end.

"Here's where things get weird. This is Bryan's knife, and it's got his blood on it. But it had been handled so much, the only distinguishable fingerprints on it were his and Mercedes. Coroner says he couldn't have killed himself." Eli grimaced. "The biggest question, though, is how this little lady got hold of it."

"Oh, Eli." Swallowing, Isabel looked at the little girl, whose downcast eyes fanned long black lashes onto cheeks the color of damask roses. Instantly her heart ached to hold this little one who'd no doubt been exposed to some terrifying events.

"Yeah." Eli's jaw worked as he gently squeezed the girl's hand. "Hatcher's been suspected of smuggling activity, and we've been watching him. We're working with DEA, Mexican police and Del Rio Homicide. I've been put in charge of protecting her, because we think she may be a witness. If she is, the murderer's looking for her. My supervisor pulled some strings with our immigration guys, and on the Mexican side, too, so I could bring her across the border."

Eli paused after having made possibly the longest speech Isabel had ever heard him make. Something in the way he held her eyes, the protective clasp of his big hand around the little girl's tiny one—

Isabel frowned. "What does all this have to do with me?"

"Sh-she needs a p-place to stay."

Isabel's gaze flew to the little girl, who let go of Eli's hand to crouch down and study the pink silk pansies on

Isabel's sandals with such innocent pleasure that Isabel closed her eyes.

But the image wouldn't fade. In that moment, her life underwent one of the irreversible changes she'd experienced only three times before. The first had been the Vacation Bible School when she'd given her heart to Jesus. The second, the night Rico asked her to marry him; the third, Danilo's birth.

She had to force herself not to run from the room. "Eli, why me?"

Chapter Two

Mortified that under pressure he'd relapsed into his childhood speech impediment, Eli tried to come up with an answer to Isabel's question. One that wouldn't make him sound crazy.

The Holy Spirit told me it should be you.

And, if he were gut-level honest, one big reason was the excuse to see Isabel every day.

"We can't spare an agent to stay with her twenty-four/seven," he finally said. "But there's a little stipend in the budget, and I thought you could use the money—"

"Eli, I'm trying to sell my house," Isabel said, as if she were explaining something to her son. "Danilo and I could be leaving Del Rio any day now. Then you'd be right back where you started."

Eli tried to gauge the depth of her protest. Her expression was troubled, but he could tell she was distracted by the child's fascination with the flowers on her shoes.

See, that was the thing. A little girl needed a woman

to care for her. A woman with an innate sense of beauty. A woman of grace and tact and spiritual wholeness, even when life crushed her.

"Okay, that's a good point," he said. "But maybe we'll nail Bryan's murderer soon, and we won't have to deal with that."

Isabel sighed. "There's another problem. I speak Spanish, but I don't know any sign language."

"She reads lips pretty well." Eli bent down to rest his hand on the little girl's head. When she looked up at him, he said carefully, *"¿Flores?"*

She gave him a wide smile and reverently touched one of the flowers on Isabel's shoes.

Eli winked at Isabel. "See?"

Isabel's smooth brow knit. "If she can do that, why can't she communicate with you? What happened when you asked her name?"

"Try it." Eli was curious to see if his instincts were correct.

Isabel rested her elbows on her knees, so that her face was close to the child's. "Isabel," she said, touching her own chest. She put a teasing finger on the little girl's nose. *"¿Como te llama?"*

The child beamed and flattened Isabel's hand. With her finger she traced a large letter M, then looked up at Isabel to see if she comprehended. When Isabel nodded, the girl finished spelling the name *Mercedes*.

Eli stared at Isabel dumbfounded. "Well I'll be…. Her name's Mercedes."

"You mean she hadn't told you that?" Isabel sat up.

"She hasn't told us *anything*," Eli said. "We've given her pencil and paper, asked her stuff, but...nothing. It's weird, because you can tell she comprehends what you're asking. Then she just gets this blank look and refuses to answer."

Isabel smiled at Mercedes, who settled cross-legged on the floor and leaned against Isabel's knee. "What else do you want to know?"

"Where she came from. Who her parents are. How she got that knife."

"I suppose I could ask." Isabel traced a gentle finger down the little girl's crooked part. "Why do you think she told *me* her name?"

Eli couldn't help wondering the same thing. His supervisor had brought in a deaf interpreter and a social worker this morning, but Mercedes had given the woman the same blank look she gave everyone else.

There was some connection with Isabel that Eli couldn't explain. He shrugged. "Maybe you look like her mother. Who knows? Listen, Isabel—" He crouched on one knee. "I'd really appreciate it if you'd take Mercedes home with you tonight. Like I said, there's even a little stipend money in the budget. You could talk to her some more, try to get her to talk back."

Isabel bit her lip. Eli could see conflicting emotions chase across her expressive face, and he knew the money had nothing to do with it. In fact, he was probably going to have to *make* her take compensation. Mercedes had obviously grabbed a piece of Isabel's tender heart.

"It might be good for Danilo to have to share me a little bit," she murmured.

"He's a good kid," Eli said. "He'll like having somebody to play with."

Isabel tipped her head and looked him in the eyes. "You think it'll just be for a day or two?"

"I'm sure of it," he said with more confidence than he felt. "So you'll do it?"

Mercedes suddenly wrapped both arms around Isabel's legs.

Eli saw Isabel's eyes fill as she laid a hand on the little girl's dark, untidy head. "I'll do it," she sighed.

"Good." Eli grinned. "I knew you would. There's just one thing though."

"I knew it." Isabel's beautifully marked brows drew together. "What's the hitch?"

"It's no big deal." But Eli found himself unable to meet her eyes. "It's just that we need to hide Mercedes until we find the killer."

"No big deal," Isabel muttered as she pulled into her driveway. "Sure, Eli. Hide an active seven-year-old in the same house with a five-year-old motormouth." The neighbors were going to notice an extra child, and how was she going to handle grocery shopping?

Her elderly Escort shuddered to a stop, and the rear passenger door burst open. Danilo, who hadn't stopped talking from the moment she'd picked him up in front of the gym, jumped out of the car and ran to open the door for Mercedes.

"Come on, Mercedes, I gotta show you the sandbox!" He grabbed his new friend by the hand and tugged.

Mercedes resisted, giving Isabel an apprehensive glance.

Isabel smiled, making a shooing motion. "Go ahead."

She needed a little time to freshen the guest room, empty the closet. There was lunch to fix, too. Danilo liked peanut butter and jelly on toast. Every day. What would Mercedes like?

Probably anything, considering the poverty across the border.

As she unlocked the side door, Isabel looked up at the light fixture, which had been left on. Had it only been this morning that Eli had been here repairing it? Seemed like a lifetime of events had transpired since then.

Which just went to prove what a true marshmallow she was. Why couldn't she just tell Eli *n-o?* He could have found somebody else to take Mercedes. There were lots of kindhearted women in their church. Women with more room, more money, less emotional baggage.

In a way, though, it was sort of flattering that he'd asked her. Eli was such a sweetie, and that boyish stammer did something to her resistance.

As she hung her purse in the laundry room and turned on the air conditioner window unit in the den, Isabel shook her head. And of course there was Mercedes herself. What mother could turn away a little girl who laid her head against your knee?

Isabel took a jar of peanut butter and a loaf of bread

out of the pantry, then peeked out the kitchen window into the backyard. Beyond the clothes flapping in the breeze, she could see the children in the sandbox. Mercedes perched with fastidious femininity on the wooden side, while Danilo knelt on all fours, plowing a truck into a sand dune. His tennis shoes and socks had been abandoned outside the box. Isabel would probably have to excavate his ears and pockets before letting him in the house.

Resigned to sweeping up at least a bucket of sand, she finished putting lunch together, then went to the door.

"Danilo!" she called. "Bring Mercedes and come in for lunch."

"Okay, Mommy," he hollered back. Momentarily both children appeared at the door. "I don't have to wash my hands," Danilo announced through the screen. "I stuck 'em in Fonzie's water bowl."

Isabel grinned. A few weeks before Rico's death, he had started feeding a mutt who'd wandered through their yard and made himself at home under the front porch. Big, ugly brown Fonzie—named after Rico's favorite *Happy Days* character—had thoroughly weaseled his way into the family.

"Nice try." She pointed at the sink. "Wash." She beckoned Mercedes, who hovered outside, and rubbed her hands together. *"Lavate,"* she said slowly, so the little girl could read the word on her lips. Then, "Wash," to demonstrate the English version.

Isabel loved to teach. In fact, she'd started college with the intention of earning her certificate, but getting pregnant right away had put an end to that. Rico had gotten bored with school and decided Border Patrol would suit him, so off they'd gone to the Academy at Glencoe. Since then she'd been so busy functioning as wife and mother, there hadn't been time to think about finishing college. And after Rico's death, she'd had all she could do to make ends meet. A talented seamstress, she'd made curtains, raised and lowered hems, sewn on buttons—boring jobs that sapped every bit of creative energy from a hobby she'd once loved.

All that was going to change, however, when she moved back to San Antonio. Her mother had promised to keep Danilo while Isabel went to college. She was going to be a teacher if it killed her.

All she had to do was sell this fixer-upper.

She gasped. She'd forgotten all about the appointment with the real estate agent this afternoon.

It was time to introduce to Danilo the concept of secrecy.

Isabel set a plate of sandwiches in the middle of her kitchen table, which served as dining room, breakfast nook, study and sewing room as the need arose. Danilo, who had long ago disdained the idea of a booster seat, hopped onto a chair with both legs folded under his bottom.

He folded his hands under his chin. "Can I say the blessing, Mommy?"

He always said the blessing, but he always asked first—a relic of the days when Rico used to take turns with him. The question never failed to tighten Isabel's throat.

"Yes, but let's get Mercedes situated first." Isabel turned to find the little girl still in the laundry room, holding a pink hand towel against her cheek. After a deep, appreciative sniff, Mercedes neatly hung the towel on its rack. She smiled and circled her palm in front of her face.

"*¿Bonita?*" Isabel guessed, nodding. Oh, dear, how was she going to communicate with this little one? How would one say "eat?" She took a stab at it, bringing bunched fingers to her mouth.

Mercedes's face lit. She rubbed her tummy.

Isabel laughed in relief. "Okay, I'm hungry, too," she said in Spanish, patting her own stomach. "Come." Offering her hand, she led Mercedes to a place at the table across from Danilo, who was now bouncing with impatience.

"Hurry, Mommy, God's waiting."

Smiling, Isabel sat at her end of the table near the bay window. "Let's pray," she said, bowing her head. Hopefully, having spent a couple of days with Benny at the orphanage, Mercedes would understand what was going on.

"Dear God, thanks for helping me write my name today."

As Danilo rambled for a couple of minutes and finally got around to thanking God for the food, Isabel couldn't help peeking. She was surprised and pleased to see Mercedes, eyes closed and hands moving, talking quite comfortably to God in her own way.

With a jolt, she realized Mercedes had pointed to her and Danilo several times.

When was the last time she'd felt like the answer to somebody's prayer? Father, help me to be a blessing to this little girl.

"Amen," said Danilo, reaching for a sandwich.

"Manners," Isabel cautioned. "Offer one to your guest first."

Danilo blinked. "Oh, yeah." He thrust the plate across the table. "Here, Mercedes. The one on top's got more jelly in it. You can have it." He looked at Isabel, who smiled in approval. She'd given up convincing him Mercedes couldn't hear his chatter.

Mercedes timidly took the top sandwich, watching for Isabel to begin eating before she took a dainty nibble. In between bites Mercedes examined the mermaid characters on her plate and cup. Someone had given them to Isabel as a baby gift before Danilo's birth, and she'd put them away in case she ever had a girl. It was good to have a use for the dishes.

"Nilo," began Isabel, "there's something I need to talk to you about."

Danilo's eyes widened. "Mrs. Logan said she wouldn't call you."

Isabel frowned. "About what?"

"About the time-out."

"And why were you in time-out?" Danilo hid behind his milk glass, but Isabel waited him out.

He emerged sporting a world-class milk mustache. "I's just talking."

"You can't talk whenever you feel like it, Danilo. That's disrespectful and disobedient."

"I'm sorry, Mommy." Danilo's big brown eyes were sorrowful. "I told Mrs. Logan I's sorry. I was telling Josh a joke. You know, what has two knees and swims?"

Isabel closed her eyes and took a deep breath. This was not going to work. Nilo couldn't *not* talk. How in the world was she going to keep Mercedes's presence a secret?

She leaned her head on her hand and regarded her son. "Okay, buddy. If Mrs. Logan forgave you, then I forgive you. But that's not what I wanted to talk to you about. It's Mercedes."

Danilo beamed at Mercedes. "*Thank* you for getting me a sister! She's way more fun than Josh's sister."

Isabel's mouth fell open. "She's not your sister! She's just going to stay with us for a couple of days while the police look for a bad man who wants to find her."

"I won't let any bad man get her," Danilo declared. "I'll put on my superhero pajamas and—"

"Honey, no. Listen, all I need you to do is not tell anybody she's staying with us."

"But why?"

The three-letter W word. Why, why, why. If she heard it once, she heard it forty times a day.

"Because…" Isabel laid both hands on the table on either side of her plate. "Because I said so."

"Not even Josh?"

"Especially not Josh."

"Not Mrs. Logan?"

Isabel firmly shook her head.

Danilo scrunched his face for a moment, then grinned. "Superheroes can't tell anybody who they are. I like secrets."

Relief washed through Isabel. "That's right. It's a secret."

"Okay." Danilo cut a Rico-like look at Isabel. "But can I at least *pretend* she's my sister?"

Pablo Medieros reracked the hundred-eighty-pound barbell he'd been bench-pressing and sat up to wipe his chest with a towel. In his opinion, the Piedras Negras Fitness Center was of barely acceptable standards, but it was the only private gym in town. His gaze touched the dusty windowsills and ceiling fans, the frayed carpet, the spiderwebs in the corners.

When Governor Avila, his boss and first cousin, won reelection this fall, his first action would be attracting businesses to the depressed cities along the border. If he brought money here, civic improvements across the state would follow.

Of course, in Pablo's opinion, the legal route wasn't always the most efficient. He didn't much care which side of the law he stepped across; after all, legality was relative.

Relative, as in family. Relative, too, depending on one's perspective.

Smiling at his own joke, Pablo walked to the locker room and extracted his cell phone from his gym bag. He punched numbers to check his messages.

"Hey, Pablo," came the rasping voice of Camino,

one of his two employees. "We found a kid who saw the little girl you're looking for, hiding out in the orphanage in St. Teresa Colony. I'd check it out for you, but the governor's got me tied up with a trip to the States this week. Don't know what you want her for, but—"

The connection disintegrated, leaving Pablo scowling.

What was the good of paying people to work for you, if they were always leaving town? On the other hand, if Avila was out of the way, Pablo would have time to do something about the mess that brat had caused.

He still couldn't believe he'd let her get away with the knife. Rage overtook him afresh, and he kicked the door of the closest locker. Scrawny little girl-child, worse than vermin. If only he'd caught her. He'd almost had her by the foot that night.

Well, it would be easy enough to take care of her at the orphanage. He'd kept an ear to the ground via a buddy in the Acuña police department. If he could get to the girl before she turned the knife in, everything would still be all right.

He calmed himself. He *would* take care of her.

Mercedes stepped out of the bathtub and let the beautiful American *señora*—Isabel—wrap her in a big fluffy towel. With delight she curled her toes into the deep pile of the yellow rug as Isabel pulled a second towel from a cabinet under the sink, then began to briskly rub Mercedes's hair.

She had never seen a place this clean. She had never *been* this clean, head to toe, and she even had her own toothbrush with a cartoon character on the handle. Danilo had shared his toothpaste, and it tasted like bubble gum.

Mercedes realized Isabel was talking to her, so she watched her lips but couldn't quite figure out what she said. Lupe had taught Mercedes a lot of English words, but she was going to have to work hard to catch up. She didn't want to miss anything Isabel said.

Isabel suddenly smiled and drew her close, wet hair and all, and Mercedes leaned in to feel the pulse of laughter against her cheek. Then Isabel set her away a bit, both hands cupping Mercedes's face, and said in careful Spanish, "I'm sorry, I forgot. Let's find you some pajamas, then we'll comb and dry your hair."

With the towel clutched around her, Mercedes followed Isabel into Danilo's room and watched her dig through a small chest of drawers. Pulling out a pair of colorful briefs, Isabel frowned and glanced at Mercedes. "Boy pants," she said with clear dissatisfaction. "We'll ask Eli to bring you some things tomorrow." Then she brightened. "I can make you a nightgown. With lace." Her eyes sparkled as she made a fluttering motion with her fingers, girl to girl.

Mercedes grinned and copied the gesture.

Oh, God had sent her to a place of richness. She had been frightened when Eli put her in the little blue car and backed away, making it clear he wasn't coming. But he'd said he would visit and bring her a doll. Mercedes didn't care so much about a doll, but if it came with Eli, then everything would be all right.

Isabel was engulfed by darkness. Standing high atop the apex of *el puente negro,* the old iron railroad bridge that arched across the Rio Grande, she knew that Piedras Negras lay to the south and Eagle Pass to the north. But with the city lights extinguished, she couldn't tell up from down, right from left.

Fear made her fingertips tingle and her stomach lurch. If she stepped an inch in any direction she would plunge into the black water. Nothing to break her fall.

Then she saw a light, two lights approaching from the American side, swinging side-to-side as if looking for something. Rico. It had to be Rico and Jack, on patrol. Illegal aliens attempted to swim across here nearly every night.

But it was late. Rico should have been home an hour ago. Anger replaced her fear. She opened her mouth to call out. If she could get Rico's attention, he'd get her down, and they could go home. Danilo missed his daddy reading a bedtime comic book story.

Her voice wouldn't come out. Mute, she watched the lights reach the cane at the edge of the water.

Suddenly the silence was broken by gunshots. Popping and pinging with obscene rhythm. Clang on metal, thud into wood. One of the lights collapsed, splintered by the cane, doused in the water.

Isabel teetered on the bridge, unable to scream, terrified beyond expression. Sweat poured in streams between her breasts, soaking her nightgown, and tears dripped off her chin.

Rico was gone. If she'd just been able to tell him one more time how much she loved him, maybe he would have come home on time.

Baby, I'm sorry I was angry. I loved you so much.

Now he would never come home, and she was going to have to stand on this bridge alone forever.

She woke up with a start, covered in sweat.

Eli bent down to ruffle the ears of Isabel's dog as he walked up her front porch steps. He'd just gotten off duty and hadn't even been home yet, but he had to find out if Mercedes had communicated anything to Isabel during the last two days.

"Sit, Fonzie," he said, snapping his fingers. The dog slurped Eli's fingers one more time and obeyed, one eye cocked for potential treats. "Dude, you are no Lassie," Eli told him as he knocked on the door.

The relaxing of Isabel's shoulders when she opened the door and scanned him from head to toe made him glad he'd changed into civilian clothes before walking down the street to her house.

She smiled. "Eli. Hi, come in." She looked beautiful as always, but there was a tired droop to her dark eyes.

"Hope my timing's not bad," he said, stepping into the tiny foyer.

"No, I'm just putting the kids to bed. Danilo's in the tub." She pushed a wavy lock of black hair behind her ear. "Did you come to check on Mercedes?"

"Not really," he replied, following her into the den. "I know you're taking good care of her. I was just wondering how, uh, communication's going."

"It's amazing what you can do with hand motions." Isabel hesitated. "Sit down, would you like something to drink?" she said in a rush as she headed for the kitchen.

"No, thanks, I just ate supper." Eli looked around and decided the leather recliner looked more comfortable than the sofa. He plopped into it with a sigh.

Isabel turned and stopped. Barefoot, dressed in a pair of white shorts and a pink knit top, she looked about fifteen years old. In a long silence, color came and went in her cheeks.

Eli swallowed. What had he done wrong? "Are you ok-k-kay, Isabel?"

She took a sudden breath. "I'm fine. I'm just—" She laughed. "Never mind. Let me just check on Danilo. I'll be right back."

She disappeared into the back of the house, leaving Eli scratching his head. "Maybe I should have asked for a root beer," he muttered.

As a series of whalelike splashes came from the bathroom, he picked up an unfinished sampler lying on the lamp table. "This precious treasure" was all it said. Eli knew nothing about sewing, but even he could see that Isabel was a gifted needlewoman. Every stitch of the elaborate border was carefully executed, and the back side of the fabric was as neat as the front.

Suddenly he was aware of Mercedes standing in the doorway. Her damp hair hung in wavy hanks around her shoulders, and she had on a pink nightie with lace edging just brushing her bare feet. He smiled as the little toes curled.

When he crooked a finger, Mercedes sidled toward him. She came as far as Isabel's mahogany rocker and sat down, where she continued to watch Eli with sober brown eyes.

Mercedes made the sign for woman, then pretty. She pantomimed sewing and brushed her hands down the front of her gown. Clearly she was proud of the garment.

"Isabel made it for you?" he guessed aloud. "Isabel?" he repeated slowly, as she watched his lips.

Mercedes nodded, beaming, and made the sign for beautiful again.

Eli grinned. "Oh, yeah. She is."

He'd love to know what was going on behind Mercedes's intelligent expression. He'd been using every spare minute to study an American Sign Language book he'd checked out of the library. This would be a good time to practice.

But before he could do more than ask Mercedes how old she was, and discover that she was seven, Isabel came back into the room with Danilo riding piggyback.

"Eli!" shouted the little boy. "Let's play baseball!"

"Maybe next time, cowboy." Eli glanced at Isabel. "It's already dark outside."

"You're on your way to bed, Nilo," said Isabel. "Tell Eli good-night." She held out a hand to Mercedes. "You, too, sweetie."

Mercedes let Isabel pull her to her feet. To Eli's astonishment, the little girl blew him a kiss before heading for the bedrooms.

Isabel's eyes widened, too, but she leaned over to let Danilo and Eli high-five over her shoulder. The subtle, spicy scent of roses, along with the sweetness of bubblegum toothpaste, gave Eli an odd, familiar pang from his childhood that made him wish he could kick the recliner back and stay indefinitely.

He suddenly understood Isabel's flustered behavior when he'd sat down in the recliner. It must have been Rico's favorite place. The husband chair. The daddy chair.

Eli jumped to his feet.

Chapter Three

Isabel looked up at Eli, noting with interest that his ears had turned scarlet. She had no idea what she'd done to make him bolt to his feet, but she knew she was glad he'd vacated Rico's chair. Trying to analyze her feelings, she decided she wasn't exactly angry. Maybe just…uncomfortable.

Aware.

A good-looking single man sitting in Rico's place seemed disloyal somehow. Because for a split second, when she'd opened her front door and found Eli standing there, she'd felt a dizzy sort of elation that he'd come by.

Danilo wrapped both arms around Isabel's neck, nearly strangling her. "Come on, horsie, back to the ranch," he said, bouncing against her back.

Isabel met Eli's blue eyes and again experienced that disconcerting feeling of falling down an elevator shaft. "I'm sorry," she stammered, "can you stay a minute? I'll be right back."

"I'll be here."

Isabel tucked Danilo in with his favorite plastic action figure, then crossed the hall to the guest room. Mercedes had climbed into bed, but the overhead light was still on. Isabel had discovered that her little guest didn't much like the dark.

Sitting on the edge of the bed, Isabel turned on the night-light and kissed Mercedes's brow. "Good night, angel," she whispered, smiling as Mercedes released a contented sigh and closed her eyes. What would it be like to have no reference of sound for the normal activities of everyday life?

Isabel flipped the wall switch off and left the door ajar so that the hall light would filter into the room, then returned to the den. She found Eli still on his feet, examining a family photo on the bookshelf beside the kitchen door.

"The obligatory Alamo picture," he commented, setting the frame back in its spot.

Isabel came to look, though of course she'd seen the photo hundreds of times. It had been taken during a visit with her parents, on a typical hot, muggy San Antonio day. Isabel had stood in front of Rico, with two-year-old Danilo perched on his dad's shoulders and pointing at the pigeons scavenging for popcorn on the sidewalk.

Isabel sighed. "I love the place, but it seemed to give Rico the creeps. I had to make him go through it with me."

Eli chuckled. "He wasn't much for history, was he?"

She looked at him in surprise. "No, he wasn't. I didn't know you knew him that well."

"We worked together off and on over the years whenever Torres had something else going on." Eli shrugged. "I'm sort of a history buff, especially World War Two."

"Really?" Isabel smiled. "I'm more into the Colonial and American Revolution eras. I was a history major until I had Danilo."

"How about that?" Eli turned to scan the bookcase. "You have any Stephen Ambrose stuff?"

"I have the Eisenhower biography." Isabel found the book and handed it to Eli. "Would you like to borrow it?"

"Sure, if you don't—" He looked at her, stricken. He'd flipped open the front cover, where Rico had inscribed "To Isabel, my one and only love. Happy Birthday."

"Eli, I don't mind." She bit her lip. "I've already read it."

He hesitated, but closed the book and tucked it under his arm. "I'll be careful with it."

"I know you will." She'd trust Eli with anything, though she had the sense to keep that information to herself. Enough emotional minefields had been crossed for one night. She stepped back. "So have you made any progress in locating Bryan Hatcher's killer?"

Eli blinked at the change of subject. "Not much. The Mexican police aren't as efficient as we'd like. I was hoping Mercedes would tell you how she got hold of that knife."

Isabel shook her head. "We've had all we can do, just taking care of the basics. She's so fragile...."

Eli released a breath. "Isabel, I don't mean to sound harsh, but that little girl is a lot tougher than most kids her age. Sooner or later we've got to push her for information."

As the widow of a border cop, Isabel knew better than most how critical time was in an investigation. Still, the idea of interrogating a traumatized seven-year-old made her sick.

"Let me show you something, Eli." Isabel led the way into the kitchen, then almost wished she'd had him wait in the den. Even standing in the doorway, Eli's tall, rangy frame seemed to fill up the little room. Putting the breakfast bar between them, she picked up a sheet of first-grade tablet paper that had been lying on the counter. "After supper, Danilo and I were working on his penmanship, and I wondered how much education Mercedes has had. I wrote her name, and she copied it beautifully."

"Let's see." Eli held out a hand.

Isabel gave him the paper and waited for his reaction.

After a moment he whistled between his teeth and looked up at Isabel. "This is unbelievable."

Using nothing but the contents of a sixteen-count Crayola box, Mercedes had turned the tails and loops of the letters of her name into a garden of exotic flowers—some of which were familiar to Isabel, and some which she suspected came from Mercedes's imagination. Subtle depth of shade gave perspective and light to the drawing, far beyond the usual ability of a seven-year-old.

Isabel spread her hands. "This little girl is something special."

Eli gave her a cautious look. "Maybe so, but—"

"There's another one." Isabel opened the drawer under the bar and extracted a second paper. She'd put it away because she didn't want Danilo to see it. She slid it across the counter toward Eli, then crossed her arms over her stomach, which suddenly hurt.

During ten years of patrolling the border, Eli had no doubt seen it all. Still, he stared speechless at the drawing for a moment. "I think we've found our witness," he finally said.

"I didn't want to believe she saw something like that."

"Did you talk to her about it?" Isabel couldn't interpret Eli's expression. He folded the piece of tablet paper and slipped it into his wallet.

"I tried. I pointed to the body and tried to say *who*— but she just looked at me like she didn't understand."

"Okay." Eli leaned over the counter and grabbed Isabel's hands. "Look, don't worry about it for now. I'll have a police artist look at it and see what they can figure out. You can keep gently questioning her, and if you see anything else…" He shrugged. "Just keep your eyes open, okay?"

Isabel didn't want to see anything else. She wanted to go back to her normal, regular life. She sighed. "All right. Eli, thanks for checking on us, but it's late and I'm tired."

He straightened, dropping her hands. "I'm sorry. I've got an early day tomorrow, too. I'll call you with any news."

* * *

At first Eli couldn't tell what had woken him up. He lifted his head and stared, bleary-eyed, at the green monster-eyes of the digital clock on the dresser. 2:00 a.m. He knew he hadn't set the alarm, because he didn't go on duty until seven.

Who was in his room playing the *Mission Impossible* theme?

Cell phone. Groaning, he sat up and rubbed his eyes. *Please, Lord, not Isabel.* He lunged for the phone. "Hello?" he croaked.

"Eli, it's Benny," said a husky feminine voice he barely recognized through a surge of static. Not Isabel. He relaxed a fraction. "I need you to come down here," she continued, her voice wobbling. "Something terrible's happened."

His hair stood on end. Bernadette Malone was the least melodramatic woman Eli had ever met.

"What's the matter?" He reached for his jeans.

She started to cry so hard he could hardly understand her. "I just found one of the children—somebody broke in— Oh, Eli she's dead—"

"Benny, whoa. *Which* child?"

"Dulce Garcia. I got up to check on the twins—they've both been running fever—" Benny gulped. "Anyway, I had the bathroom light on so I could read the thermometer, and I noticed Dulce was lying on her back. She always sleeps on her stomach, curled up in a knot. I put my hand on her forehead out of habit, and she was cold, I don't know how long she'd been—" Benny's voice disintegrated into sobs.

"Benny, listen." Eli felt like throwing up. He had his jeans on, and he dug a T-shirt out of a drawer. "Had she been sick?"

"Eli, the window screen over her bed is cut. The air conditioner's been out, and we haven't had the money to fix it—"

"You've called an ambulance? The police?"

"No, I wanted you to come first. I don't trust them, they were out here asking questions a couple of days ago—"

"Questions? About what?"

"About Mercedes. When I realized they didn't know you'd taken her, I played dumb."

"Good girl. I'm working with one guy that I trust over there. Nobody else is in the loop." Gathering his thoughts, Eli started to holster his gun, then remembered he couldn't take it across the border. "Listen, I'm on my way. Don't go anywhere."

"Where would I go?" Benny asked. "Hurry, Eli."

The connection ended.

Praying for direction, Eli clipped the phone to his belt and headed for his Jeep. As he drove across the international bridge that led to the Border Patrol checkpoint station, he reviewed what he knew.

A child murdered in her sleep in a Mexican orphanage. A child bearing a close resemblance to a mysterious little girl who had appeared there two days ago. A little girl gifted with extraordinary artistic talent, and who happened to be carrying a murder weapon.

And two years ago, Eli had decided to get involved in his church's mission outreach to that orphanage.

Nothing was accidental. In the same way he'd sensed the connection with Mercedes, Eli knew God had chosen him uniquely for this task.

If he'd learned anything from his father's fall from grace, it was that everyone had the capacity for good or evil. And sometimes small choices led a man toward one or the other.

Because of DEA connections through Border Patrol, he had personal experience with the dark underpinnings of the drug smuggling and prostitution rings on both sides of the border. As much as he wanted to deny it, instinct told him that there was a connection between Mercedes and that darkness.

Her drawing, which he still had in his wallet, made him almost sure of it. He'd studied it carefully when he came home from Isabel's house. Eli was no child psychologist, but there had to be significance to the sinister red-and-black hues, the bloody slashes across a grotesquely human form in the center of the picture.

The most curious component of the drawing, in Eli's mind, was an element like water drops in the foreground. Did it represent tears? Rain? He tried to remember if it had been storming the night Bryan Hatcher died. He didn't think so.

Making up his mind to interview Mercedes as soon as possible, he pulled into the small parking lot reserved for Border Patrol agents at the checkpoint. Better connect with his supervisor before heading over to Mexico.

"Carmichael, you're not on until seven. Where's your

uniform?" Agent Dean looked up from his usual mountain of paperwork.

"I'll be back later in uniform. Just wanted you to know I'm headed over to the orphanage in St. Teresa Colony. A child was killed under suspicious circumstances, and the house mother is a friend, so I'm on my way to check it out." Eli hesitated over how much to tell his boss. "It may have something to do with the little deaf girl we brought over a couple days ago."

Dean's language disintegrated into curses. "I still don't think that was a good idea. I know you're working with Del Rio homicide on the Hatcher case, but if we keep interfering in every Mexican investigation, trouble's bound to escalate."

Eli buttoned up a disrespectful retort. Less than a month ago, Dean had been promoted from a desk job in Dallas. The man had yet to figure out how to connect events in Acuña and Del Rio.

Eli shrugged. "Benny Malone is American, and I promised I'd help her sort the situation out. I'll be back in uniform as quick as I can."

Dean stared Eli down before reluctantly nodding. "We're two men short on your shift as it is, Carmichael. Don't mess around and get yourself written up."

Eli's rare temper flared. Everybody in the agency knew what his father had done, but so far he'd never heard a word of blame attached to either himself or his brother, Owen. Maybe he was reading too much into Dean's words, but there was something needle-sharp buried in the admonition.

Not trusting himself to answer, Eli gave a jerky nod, turned on his heel, and left the building.

When the phone rang, Isabel was in the attic, knee-deep in dust, spiderwebs and memories. Naturally, she had forgotten to bring the handset up.

She leaned over to poke her head through the opening into the hallway. "Danilo! Will you answer the phone for Mommy?"

"Sure!" he caroled. Isabel could hear his bare feet pattering across the hardwood floor in the living room, and a distinct skid when he reached the kitchen tile. "Valenzuela residence." They'd practiced answering the phone off and on for the past month or so. He was actually getting pretty good at it.

Danilo came back down the hall. "She can't come to the phone right now. She's up in the attic, bowling."

"Danilo! Bring me that phone right now!"

Her son blinked up at her with the handset clutched to the side of his face. "But you said to stay off the ladder."

"That's right. I did." Frustrated, Isabel swiped a dusty hank of hair behind her ear. "Stay right there. I'm coming down."

"Never mind," Danilo said into the phone. "Here she comes." He paused and listened. "No, I'm through with school for today. I'm playing with—" He gulped as Isabel held out a hand for the phone. "Uh-oh, here's Mom. 'Bye, Eli."

"Eli!" Isabel's breath came quickly, both from her

precipitate trip down the ladder and from the sound of the low chuckle rumbling in her ear. "What are you doing?"

"I might ask you the same thing. Bowling in the *attic*?"

"I wasn't bowling. I just needed to get some stuff ready for a yard sale."

Truthfully, she had no intention of selling Rico's bowling ball, not now. She'd opened the leather bag and rotated the ball until she could stick her fingers in the holes. The sensation of holding hands with her husband had nearly undone her.

Isabel sniffed and swallowed a fresh wad of tears.

Eli must have heard the tremor in her voice. He was quiet for a moment, then said gently, "I'll come over this afternoon and help you with the heavy stuff. I have to talk to you about something anyway."

Anxiety clutched her stomach. "What's the matter?"

He answered her question with one of his own. "Where's your houseguest?"

"She and Danilo are playing dolls." Isabel caught her son's outraged look and grinned. "Well, she's playing dolls. *He's* actually saving the planet."

"Good. Keep them both indoors until I get there."

"Eli, what's going—"

The dial tone buzzed in her ear. She pushed the "cancel" button and gave Danilo a distracted frown. What on earth had happened now?

Isabel barely had time to brush the cobwebs out of her hair and wash her hands before Eli arrived. In uniform and as usual neat as a pin, he removed his hat as he stepped into the foyer. The sober line of his mouth sent the butterflies in Isabel's stomach chasing one another.

"Let's go in the kitchen so we can talk," she suggested, looking around to make sure Danilo was out of earshot.

Eli followed her into the kitchen. "What have you been doing today?"

Isabel pulled out a chair for Eli, then seated herself across from him. "I've been sewing all morning, then once Danilo got home…Eli, what's the matter?"

He laid his hat carefully on the table, avoiding her eyes as if he didn't know how to start. "We're going to have to be a lot more careful with Mercedes."

Isabel took a sharp breath. "If you don't tell me *right now* what's going on, I'm going to have to hurt you."

A smile cracked Eli's grim expression, then instantly disappeared. "Benny Malone called me in the middle of the night to tell me somebody broke into the orphanage and smothered Dulce Garcia with a pillow."

Isabel clapped her hand over her mouth to muffle a shriek.

Eli leaned across the table to grab her other hand. "Hold on. Yeah, it's bad. And I'm afraid it means somebody knows Mercedes saw something dangerous."

Isabel fought to get her breath back. "Why do you say that?"

"Benny said the Mexican police were back asking more questions about her. Word has gotten out that she was there." Eli's big shoulders shifted uncomfortably. "And we can't overlook the fact that Dulce was the same age and size as Mercedes."

"I just—I can't believe it." Isabel crushed Eli's hand. She wanted to get up and grab the little girl into her arms. She wanted to take her son away from this violent place.

Eli gazed at Isabel with bloodshot blue eyes underscored by dark shadows. "I spent the wee hours of the morning with the Acuña police. The officer who questioned Benny wasn't on the force. The guy's disappeared." His jaw shifted. "I'm sure glad Mercedes is with you."

Isabel closed her eyes to shut out his obvious meaning. "So am I, but—"

Old fears clamored for space in her brain. The night Rico died replayed in glaring detail: Border Patrol personnel banging on the door, waking her from a profound sleep. Danilo crying out at the noise, clinging to her. The hideous ride to the hospital in a patrol car. Rico's partner, covered in bloodstains, trying to hold her.

The sight of her husband's still face and broken body.

Isabel shuddered. If she continued to harbor this little girl, her son could be in danger.

Dear Father, please don't put me through this again.

"Isabel." Eli's voice drew her back from the darkness. She opened her eyes to his compassionate gaze. "I'll watch over you. We'll catch this guy."

Isabel snatched her hand away from Eli. Every instinct of self-preservation told her to send Mercedes away and follow through with her plans to leave Del Rio. In her circumstances, nobody would blame her. Eli might be disappointed in her, but he'd figure something out. It was his job.

But just then she felt a small hand on her forearm and looked around to see button-bright dark eyes sparkling behind her shoulder. Mercedes stood there dressed in a pair of Danilo's shorts and a top Isabel had pieced together out of scraps from somebody's yellow bridesmaid dress. The little girl gave Isabel a shy smile and thrust a fistful of dandelion blossoms under her chin.

"Oh, sweetheart," Isabel breathed, "how beautiful. Thank you." She signed the words and kissed Mercedes's cheek. How could she possibly turn this child away? Drawing Mercedes into her lap and snuggling her close, Isabel ruefully met Eli's eyes. "What exactly do you want us to do?"

"Have any of your neighbors seen Mercedes? Made comments about her?"

She shook her head. "I have a niece about her age, and we're sticking close to the house."

"Good. Then Mercedes should be safe, because we're letting it out that she was the victim last night." Eli took a deep breath. "The sad fact is that nobody will miss one little Mexican street kid. We'll just bury Dulce quietly and keep watch."

All kinds of objections came to Isabel's mind. "How much longer do you think it will take? Danilo won't be out of school for another two weeks. So far he understands we're playing the 'keep a secret' game—but sooner or later he's bound to slip."

Eli frowned. "I think you'd better pull him out of school."

"But that would cause even more comment!"

"He's only in kindergarten, right? Two weeks won't hurt anything. You can say he's sick."

"But that would be a lie!"

"Isabel. We're talking about this child's *life*. I've already l-lost one—"

The slight crack in Eli's voice wrecked Isabel's tenuous grip on her composure. She stared at him, tears pouring down her cheeks and dripping onto the top of Mercedes's head. "I'll do whatever I have to do, you know I will. But Eli, I'm so scared. This is way over my head."

Eli's boyish face hardened. "I'd give anything to change what's happened. But I can't. I don't know why God's allowed this, but I told you I'm not leaving you alone. When I'm not on duty I'll be here, and when I'm working I'll have somebody watching you."

Isabel found herself drawing strength from those steady eyes. "Can I call my friend Pam and ask her to pray for me?"

He hesitated, then shook his head. "Not a good idea. But we could pray together right now, if you want to."

The idea was somehow startling, but Isabel didn't have the heart to refuse. When she nodded, Eli came around the table and knelt beside Isabel's chair. He clasped both his big warm hands around hers, smiled at Mercedes, and bowed his head.

"Father, Isabel and I come to You and bring You our worry and fear. I pray You'll work in this bad situation for Your glory. Please help me and the other guys find Bryan's killer, and protect Mercedes until we do. Give

Isabel the wisdom she needs to communicate with Mercedes and keep out of sight. You know what's best, and You can meet our needs. We love You and thank You in Jesus's name. Amen."

Isabel had no words to pray, so she just whispered "Amen."

No turning back now.

Mercedes could tell Isabel was upset without looking at her face. The dandelions had been crushed in her hands, releasing a bitter smell into the room, and the soft arms around her were tight and almost uncomfortable. Eli's blue eyes were focused on Isabel, but Mercedes could tell he was worried about something.

He had mentioned Mercedes's name twice as he prayed, though she couldn't understand much of the rest of it. By now she and Danilo understood each other pretty well, but the adults tended to use big words she didn't know.

She knew both Isabel and Eli wanted to know about the knife. She still wasn't sure why she'd taken it. Knowing Pablo wanted it back terrified her, and she'd nearly flung it into a pile of garbage on the way to the mission.

But giving it to Eli had been the right thing to do. Something had whispered it would be all right when he'd held out his hand for it and smiled at her with those kind eyes.

Mercedes looked up at Isabel and flinched at the sight of her tears. She should never had drawn that picture. It made Isabel worry more than she already did.

And there was no way she was going to say anything more about it. Pablo would squash her like a bug if she ever did. Look what he'd done to Lupe.

Chapter Four

"Looks like the motion sensor sent us out here chasing cows again." Eli lowered his binoculars, his stomach lurching as the chopper suddenly swooped so close to the ground that he could see an armadillo waddling into the brush.

Owen brought the helicopter into flamboyant hover, then lifted his own glasses to scan the scraggly landscape. "Your tax dollars at work." He blew out such a loud breath that Eli winced. "So how's Artemio coming with finding your getaway car?"

"I think it's a lost cause. Do you know how many brown Ford LTDs are parked on the side of the road in Mexico?"

Owen grinned. "Everybody knows they migrate south for the summer. What about the autopsy report? Is it in yet?"

"Suffocation. Nothing we didn't know. But the coroner says the tests were inconclusive and we can't be certain there was foul play." Eli forestalled his brother's out-raged response. "Callous, I know. Look, I'm disgusted, too. We're just going to have to do our own legwork."

"You know I'll help however I can." Owen turned the chopper and headed back to the station. "Especially now that Benny's involved."

"Speaking of lost causes."

Owen shook his blond head. "She's choosy. I like that in a woman."

"I hate to rain on your parade, but Benny's made it perfectly clear she has no intention of dating anybody. Especially cowboy helicopter jockeys."

"Faint heart never won fair lady."

Eli chuckled. "Storm the walls and fall into the moat. The story of your life."

"Like yours is going so well." Owen threw Eli a side-long look. "How're you doing with the lovely Isabel?"

"I'm making progress."

Owen gave Eli a "yeah, right" look. "You haven't even asked her out, have you?"

"Not yet."

"Why not?"

Eli shrugged. "She's still in love with her husband." He hadn't even been able to bring himself to open the Eisenhower book. Lying on his nightstand, it taunted him with the awareness of that inscription on the title page. *To Isabel, my one and only.*

Did a woman ever get over that kind of love?

Owen took the helicopter into another breath-steal-ing dive. "You are such a chicken."

"Shut up, Owen, you don't know what you're talking about. I'm not the Casanova you *think* you are." Eli folded his arms. "I wouldn't know where to start."

"Well, to begin with you could do something a little more romantic than cut her grass. She probably thinks of you as her yard boy."

"She *needs* me to cut her grass. Danilo's not big enough yet."

Owen made a rude noise. "Okay, so you keep cutting the grass, but you take her flowers or something, too."

The idea of paying a florist good money for something that would die within forty-eight hours pained Eli's soul. But he remembered the expression on Isabel's face when Mercedes had handed her a handful of weeds. "I'll think about it," he mumbled.

At this major concession, Owen grinned. "Good. Class dismissed. There will be a test."

"All right, professor." Eli sighed. "Now see if you can set this bird down without making me lose my breakfast."

"Mommy, I'm tired of making *W*s. Can I write a letter?"

Isabel snipped a thread on the gown she had been hemming. "Let me see your work, sweetie."

Danilo shoved his tablet across the kitchen table and began a rhythmic tap with his chunky pencil and a ruler. Isabel knew she'd have to find an outlet for all his pent-up energy soon, or he was going to drive her crazy. Maybe drum lessons.

Isabel glanced at Mercedes, who was tackling a page full of subtraction problems, tongue between her teeth. As much as she was growing to love the little girl, Isabel's nerves were fraying. They hadn't been to church in three weeks, and she missed the fellowship.

She had called Pamela Hatcher, offering the excuse of a sick child for missing Bryan's funeral. No matter what Eli said, the lie made her uncomfortable, and Pamela's understanding had made Isabel feel even worse. She'd prayed over the phone with Benny Malone, too, after little Dulce's death. Benny had promised to come for a visit soon, but volunteer relief for orphanage housemothers was hard to come by. In fact, Isabel herself had been the only person to sub for Benny in quite some time.

With a sigh, Isabel confiscated Danilo's ruler and stuck it in her sewing basket. "Your W's are pretty good, except they need to touch bottom." She demonstrated.

"You mean like in Josh's swimming pool?" Danilo gave Isabel one of his patented cajoling looks. "Would you write my letter for me? I don't spell good."

"I don't spell *well*," she corrected. "Who do you want to write to? Your nana?" Isabel hadn't talked to her mother in over a week. She really should call.

"No, I want to write to Daddy."

Isabel jabbed herself with the needle. "What?" She quickly put her finger into her mouth.

"I said—"

"I heard you." She smiled at Mercedes, who had looked up from her drawing. Isabel saw that Danilo's smooth brow had furrowed at her sharp tone. She took a breath. "Baby, Daddy's in heaven."

"I know. But he could look over my shoulder and read my letter."

Isabel fought to maintain her composure. Explaining death to a five-year-old had its challenges. She laid the dress, needle and thread down in her lap. "Okay. What do you want to say?"

Danilo beamed and handed Isabel his pencil. "'Dear Daddy, I miss you.'"

Isabel turned to a fresh page in the tablet and wrote. *Oh, Lord Jesus, this is hard.* She looked at her son. "Got it. Now what?"

"'But Mommy and me are doing great and we even have a new sister.' I know," he added when Isabel opened her mouth to object. "My *pretend* sister."

Isabel wrote the sentence, looking up when Mercedes put a hand on her arm. The little girl's face was lit like a May sunbeam. Isabel continued to be staggered by how quickly she had learned to read English.

"Mom!" Danilo tapped Isabel's shoulder. "I'm not finished."

"Okay, buddy. What else?"

Danilo screwed up his face in thought. "'We have to stay in the house a lot, but we get to play 'Sets' and Eli comes to see us, so I don't care.'"

For some reason, this confession was nearly impossible for Isabel to put on paper. A vivid mental image of his sky blue eyes had her bearing down on the pencil to keep it from trembling in her hand.

"One more thing." Danilo bounced on his knees. "'I'm gonna play T-ball this summer, and Eli said he'd teach me how to hit a home run. Love, Nilo.'"

Isabel bit her lip. "Wouldn't you like to sign it yourself?"

"No thanks. Can I go play in the sandbox?"

A little while later, having sent the children outside, Isabel looked up at a tap on the back door. She laid down her sewing and walked into the laundry room.

"Eli!" She caught herself just short of flinging her arms around him. Isabel backed toward the kitchen, and he came in, wearing jeans and a T-shirt that said "Two lefts don't make a right, but three do." She laughed. "Are you moving in?"

He looked down as if he'd forgotten the overflowing grocery sacks in both hands. "Oh. I went by the HEB and picked up a few things for you."

"Did you leave anything in the store?" she teased. "Come in. Let's see."

He clunked his load down on a counter and backed away. "You said you needed the basics…."

Isabel pulled out a half-gallon container of peanut butter and smiled. "This ought to last us a while."

"I always liked peanut butter when I was a kid."

"Danilo does, too. I'll make some cookies this afternoon."

Eli grinned. "I knew this was a good idea."

Isabel unloaded a huge can of baked beans, a six-pound package of ground beef, three boxes of Cap'n

Crunch— "It was on sale," Eli said sheepishly—and a towering stack of frozen pizzas.

Isabel hid a smile. "I hope I have room for all those in my freezer."

"I'll eat three of them tonight, myself." Eli opened Isabel's pantry and looked over his shoulder. "I thought I'd stay with the kids and let you go shopping or whatever. You must be getting tired of staying home."

Isabel sighed. "You have no idea. I know it's silly, but I've felt like I've been in prison."

Eli folded his arms. "I'm really sorry. I didn't think it would take this long." He hesitated. "Owen and I did some surveillance in his chopper yesterday."

"Really? Any news?"

He shook his head. "Just routine illegal crossings, which of course we had to follow up on."

"What about the orphanage? Is Benny safe there?"

"Acuña PD is still keeping an eye on her. They did find somebody in the neighborhood who saw a brown LTD speeding away about 1:00 a.m. the night Dulce died. And no—" he anticipated her question "—they haven't nailed a good suspect. The car was stolen, but they're checking on every possibility."

"Eli, you know I'm glad to help, but the longer Mercedes stays here the harder it's going to be for her to leave when the time comes."

Truth be told, Isabel knew *she* was the one who'd have a hard time. She looked out the window. The children were taking turns on the swing Rico had hung on one end of the clothesline. Right now Danilo was pushing Mercedes, who hung backward with her long, black hair trailing in the dust. Isabel smiled. Time to wash heads tonight.

Eli was silent for such a long time that Isabel turned to make sure she hadn't offended him. She found him standing beside the table, holding the letter she and Danilo had written to Rico.

He looked stricken.

He met her eyes. "Isabel, I'm sorry. I have no intention of taking Rico's place."

There were so many implications to that statement that Isabel hardly knew where to begin. "I know that. And I don't think Danilo feels that way, either." She looked away. "He's only five, Eli. He enjoys having an adult male to play with."

"Maybe that's all it is." Eli didn't sound convinced.

"Listen, if you're worried that he's getting too attached to you, I'll explain you're busy and—"

"No! Don't do that." Eli laid the tablet on the table and approached Isabel. "I get a kick out of the superhero stuff, and I *offered* to teach him to hit a baseball off a tee." He stopped close to her, resting a hand above her head on the pantry door. "It just didn't occur to me that it might upset you."

Isabel looked up at him, and something stung her heart, something sweet and caring in those blue eyes. "I'm not upset."

But she was. Upset and confused and wishing for her mother to talk to. Rico had never towered over her this way, had never worried about upsetting her, had never been to the grocery store for her.

As if sensing her discomfort, Eli stepped back and sighed. "I bought Danilo a T-ball set. It's out in the car."

"What do you mean, you offed the wrong kid?" Pablo snarled into the phone.

He'd stepped outside the back door of Universidad Autónoma's new administration building auditorium, where the governor was officiating at the ribbon-cutting ceremony. Pablo's phone had buzzed against his hip as he stood guard backstage, and the caller ID told him he'd better take the call.

Now he wished he could use the muscles he worked so hard to maintain, in order to smash the already broken nose of José Camino. Instead he was stuck here in Ciudad Juarez, listening to his boss drone on about education, while Camino fouled up his business back in Acuña.

He gripped the cell phone so hard he heard it crack. "How do you know this?"

"Last night I had a beer with my friend in the Acuña police. The American Border Patrol came asking questions, and he thought it strange they were interested in a worthless little girl named Dulce Garcia." Camino sounded offended. "If you'd given me better information—"

"I told you she's deaf, I told you exactly what she looks like!" Pablo cursed Camino to relieve his feelings. "I cannot believe you were so stupid."

"I can't snatch a kid during the day, when they're all

guarded like that. And how can I tell which skinny little girl with long black hair is deaf, when they're all sound asleep?" Camino's voice had risen to a defensive shout.

Pablo glanced at his watch. He had to get back to the ceremony before the governor looked around and found his head of security missing. "Did you at least search the room for the knife?"

"Yeah. It's not there. At least I don't think so. I had to leave because one of the other kids started to wake up."

Pablo crunched his knuckles. "All right. Keep your ears open and see if somebody will tell you what happened to the other girl. The one we're actually looking for."

Sarcasm apparently rolled right off Camino's back. "Will do."

The connection ended, and Pablo reentered the auditorium's dark backstage area, not a moment too soon. Applause rippled as the governor smiled and waved before exiting the stage.

As Pablo followed his boss into the limo, he mulled over his problem. If the Americans were interested in the child's death, maybe they had something to do with Mercedes's disappearance. Pablo settled back in his seat. He could suck up to his boss in his sleep, so he had no trouble glibly praising the governor's enlightening speech while formulating his own plan of action.

Mentally he began to review his contacts across the border.

Consulting her list, Isabel turned her shopping cart down the pet supplies aisle. The discount store on Saturday afternoon was a zoo, but Fonzie was in desperate need of flea shampoo. Maybe Eli wouldn't mind—

She halted the thought right there. She had gotten way too dependent on Eli lately. It was time Danilo learned to bathe the dog.

And it won't kill you to get wet and soapy, either, she told herself.

She found the shampoo and wandered down a couple more aisles until she located the cosmetics. What a luxury to stand here and look to her heart's content, without having to worry about her little sidekick knocking over endcaps, hang gliding on the buggy or initiating conversations with strangers.

She'd left Eli out in the backyard with the children, demonstrating proper batting stance. The miniature bat looked like a matchstick in Eli's big hands, and powerful muscles bulged all over the place as he swung it. Feeling oddly out of breath, Isabel had scurried for the carport.

Life right now was just very…weird. She felt caught between a desire to rewind time back to the way it had been before Rico died, and an even more desperate urge to move on to whatever the Lord had next for her. The patches of grief had become fewer and farther between, but there was certainly no peace in her life.

That had to be wrong.

She picked up a bottle of rose-scented shower gel, opened it and sniffed. What was Eli's favorite scent?

The thought was so shocking that she capped the bottle, tossed it into the cart and hustled down the aisle.

What is the matter with you, Isabel Valenzuela? Have you lost your mind? She most definitely needed to get out more often.

At the end of the aisle she nearly bowled over an elegant, silver-haired lady in white slacks and a fuchsia silk top.

"Pamela!" Isabel gasped. "I'm so sorry! I wasn't watching where I was going."

Pamela Hatcher laughed and pushed her cart side-by-side with Isabel's. "No harm done. In fact, I was hoping I would *run into* you somewhere."

Isabel giggled. "Ow. Bad, Pam. I'm sorry we haven't been able to get together to pray lately." She hesitated. "I've had a lot of sewing deadlines." That was certainly the truth. *Lord, please don't let me have to lie to my friend.*

"I know." Pamela sighed and fiddled with the clasp of her handbag. "I didn't want to bother you. But I've really needed some prayer support."

"I'm sorry," Isabel could only repeat. She touched Pamela's hand briefly. "I know you miss Bryan. I can't imagine."

Pamela's bright green eyes watered. "I have a feeling you can, just a bit. But we always think our children are going to outlive us."

"And our husbands," Isabel added uncomfortably. How many times over the past year had she railed at God for taking Rico long before his time? "I wouldn't have survived this year without my church family. If anything were to happen to Danilo I think I'd go over the edge."

"I know. It's so hard when your children grow up, and you lose all control of their lifestyles. Rand keeps wondering if he'd spent more time with Bryan…" Pamela took a shaky breath and seemed to push away her melancholy. "So where is your little guy this afternoon? Did he spend the weekend with your parents?" She glanced at Isabel's cart.

Isabel couldn't control a small, guilty start. "He's home with a babysitter."

Pamela lowered her voice. "How is he handling your relationship with Eli Carmichael?"

The breath left Isabel's lungs. "What are you talking about?" Her voice came out in a strangled whisper.

"It's not any big secret, is it?" Pamela leaned in. "I started to come over last week, but I saw him leaving your house and changed my mind."

Blood rushed to Isabel's cheeks. "Eli has been—he *is* my friend, that's all." Maybe a hit-and-run with the shopping carts would have circumvented this situation. She looked at her watch. "Oh, my, look at the time, I've got to get back—"

Pamela's eyes lit. "Eli's the sitter, isn't he? Oh, Isabel, I think this is wonderful. You shouldn't be embarrassed."

"Pam, I promise you—"

"Okay, I won't tell anybody. But he's the cutest thing, he'll be perfect for you. He's never been married, but of course you know that. Rand and I both noticed the way his eyes follow you at church." Pamela reached out and impulsively hugged Isabel, who stood stiff as a store mannequin, wishing some wild woman would come by and run over *her* with a shopping cart.

Before she could protest further, Pamela let her go, promising to call so they could set up a lunch date, and moved off toward electronics.

"Oh, no!" Isabel put her hand to her mouth. "What if she says something to Eli?"

Eli hated himself for not telling Isabel his true reason for keeping the kids tonight, but he needed to talk to Mercedes alone. He should have known Isabel would be too tenderhearted to press the little girl for information. So it was up to him to pry it out of her.

Leaving Danilo wrestling with the dog, he walked over to push Mercedes in the swing. She gave him that gap-toothed grin over her shoulder, and leaned back to pump the swing higher. In many ways she seemed utterly fearless.

Eli wondered what went on in her imaginative little brain when she was alone in the dark. Did she have nightmares about bloody knives?

Knowing he couldn't put this off any longer, he grabbed the swing's chains to stop it. He went around to crouch in front of Mercedes.

She tipped her head, smiling at him, and he saw that the scab on her knee had fallen off, leaving a rough white scar. Other than that, she looked as happy and secure as any well-cared-for seven-year-old. He was going to take her back to scars on her soul even more permanent than the one on her knee.

Eli had thought this over a lot. Easy does it, he told himself. With two fingers he pointed to her eyes, then touched his own lips. "Watch me speak," he said in Spanish.

Mercedes grinned and nodded.

Eli continued in her native language, though he knew she understood a lot of English by now. He didn't want there to be any misunderstanding. "Tell me about this picture." He opened his wallet and removed the bloody drawing.

Mercedes's expression changed. Her smile fled, and darkness that had nothing to do with color filled her eyes. She shook her head and did something with her hands that he couldn't understand.

Okay, back to yes-and-no questions. "Is this something you saw?"

Predictably, she shook her head.

"Mercedes, I won't let anybody hurt you again. If you saw someone hurt another person, you have to tell me so I can—" He realized she had closed her eyes, and he didn't know what to do to make her look at him. He gently took her face in his hands and kissed her forehead. "Never mind," he whispered to nobody in particular.

Now what was he going to do?

Chapter Five

"Die, you villain!" The blue-and-red pajama-clad superhero aimed gloved wrists at his nemesis, two fingers folded into his palms as he sprayed sound effects. "You'll never hurt my girlfriend while I'm around!"

"I'll get you someday!" With a groan that clearly indicated lifeblood pouring from his villainous body, Eli sank to the carpet. He writhed in mortal anguish, then lay twitching.

"You'll never escape me!" declared the hero, stomping a light-up sandal into Eli's solar plexus.

"Oof!" Eli involuntarily rolled over.

Danilo frowned. "It's not funny, Mercedes. He's the bad guy!"

"I'll show you a bad guy." Eli sat up to pull Danilo down for a tickle. The boy giggled and squirmed, while Mercedes jumped on Eli's back. "Hey, no fair, two against one!"

He reached around to pull Mercedes into his arms,

falling back against the living room carpet. Fonzie took that as an invitation to join the game, and Eli got his face washed by a long, pink, slobbery tongue.

"What is that dog doing in the house?"

Isabel's outraged cry from the kitchen doorway rang the bell on the impromptu wrestling match.

After a moment of startled, guilty silence, Danilo scrambled to his feet. "Mommy!" He ran to throw his arms around Isabel's legs. Fonzie slunk off behind the recliner, and Mercedes shrank against Eli, eyes worried.

Isabel's expression settled into confusion as she ruffled Danilo's hair. She sniffed. "What is that smell?"

Eli sat up, hugging Mercedes. "That would be wet dog."

"Fonzie took a shower." Danilo beamed up at his mother.

"He took a—*what?*"

"You said he couldn't come in the house 'cause he was dirty, so we put him in the shower."

"I bet he loved that," Isabel said, a reluctant grin tugging at her mouth.

"I think he actually enjoyed it," Eli said, smiling down at Mercedes, whose anxious expression lightened. "He seems to be part Lab. They're big water dogs." Noticing the bags that Isabel carried, he jumped up, carefully setting Mercedes on her feet. "Here, let me get those for you."

Isabel's cheeks turned rosy. "No, I'll just go put them in my room." She backed away from him, beckoning to Mercedes. "Come with me, darlin'?"

Mercedes ran to take Isabel's hand, leaving Eli to settle on the floor, flanked by the dog and the boy.

Danilo yawned. "I don't want to take a bath," he said, rubbing his eyes.

"Me, neither," said Eli. "But girls kinda like it when you don't stink."

"Why?"

"Don't know." Eli gently scrubbed his knuckles against the top of the dark head tucked under his arm. "One of those mysteries of life."

"I already got my pajamas on."

"Yeah." Eli watched as Danilo fell asleep right before his eyes. He smiled. Poor little guy hadn't even had any supper. Eli wondered if Isabel would wake him up to feed him and bathe him. Isabel was a world-class mother. Likely, a little stink wouldn't faze her.

When she came back, accompanied by Mercedes dressed in the pink nightgown, her eyes softened. "The hero falls victim to the Sandman."

"Yeah, we pretty much wore each other out." Eli rubbed the back of his neck. "Want me to put him in bed for you?"

"Not until he's good and asleep." Isabel sat down in the rocker with Mercedes in her lap. "I really appreciate you giving me a hand on your day off. Beyond the call of duty."

"Not really. It's in my best interests to keep you happy."

Isabel looked self-conscious. "You may not think so when I tell you who I ran into in the soap aisle."

"Uh-oh. That doesn't sound good."

"I told you I wanted to call Pamela Hatcher. She apparently came by the other night when you were here so late."

Eli frowned. "She was watching your house?"

"Eli, we're good friends. Prayer partners, and we talk nearly every day. When she didn't hear from me and couldn't get me on the phone—well, she drove over here to check on me. Pam saw you leaving."

Eli watched the deep lids flicker to hide Isabel's dark eyes. "And this is a problem because…"

"Because she thinks we—she thinks you and I are—" Isabel circled her hand and gave Eli a helpless look. "I know that sounds crazy, and I tried to tell her so, but she wouldn't listen."

Eli couldn't tell if Isabel was angry or simply incredulous. Clearly she had no clue about his feelings, which meant he must be a pretty good actor. He felt his way along in this embarrassing conversation.

"You know what," he said, "that may not be a bad thing. In fact, I wish I'd thought of it myself."

Isabel's lips parted. "Huh?"

He shrugged. "Somebody's got to be watching out for you and Mercedes, and I'd feel better if it were me. If it will cause less speculation among your friends, we can let them think we're…involved."

"But it's not true!"

The words sat out there between them as Eli considered his response. "We've talked about it before," he said carefully. "We can't keep Mercedes safe if people know she's here. A little bit of prevarication is necessary."

"I know, but not about—" Isabel looked around a bit wildly. "You know."

Eli's gaze fell on the Alamo photo. "Isabel, you've been a widow for nearly two years. Nobody would fault you for starting to date again."

Stroking Mercedes's hair, Isabel closed her eyes. "I'm just not ready yet."

Another awkward silence. "Okay, look, I understand. I really do. But the bottom line of this situation is Mercedes. She needs both of us." He watched Isabel's arms tighten around the little girl. "Look at me, Isabel," he said softly.

She obeyed, eyes dark and wary.

Eli smiled. "I promise just to be your friend." But he wasn't sure he could keep that promise. More than halfway across the bridge in love with Isabel, he couldn't figure out how to get back.

"I could really use a friend," she said on a sigh. "I just never imagined it would be—" She stopped, looking self-conscious.

"Me?" Eli supplied. Dennis Carmichael's son falling in love with Rico Valenzuela's widow. Some might say God had a cruel sense of humor. Eli rejected the thought. "I happen to think there's a reason we've been thrown together like this."

"I don't know." Isabel shook her head. "Ever since you came over that day, asking me to meet Mercedes, I started having nightmares again."

"Nightmares? You mean about Rico?"

"Yes." Isabel's voice was low and strained. "Every

night I dream about that place over in Eagle Pass where he died."

Eli wanted to move close to her and take her in his arms. He didn't dare. Instead he looked at her steadily, keeping his voice even. "Have you talked to a counselor? The pastor?"

Her eyes widened. "No! I don't want anybody to think I'm...crazy."

"Isabel, you're not crazy. Even though I wasn't there, I dream about that scene, too—or I used to. Sometimes I'm jerking the gun out of my father's hand, sometimes I step in front of the bullet." He shook his head. "The counselor said that's normal."

"You went to a counselor?" Isabel tipped her head. "You've never seemed to let what happened bother you."

"Oh, I'm bothered all right." Eli looked away. "Some days it's all I can do to look you in the eye."

"Oh, Eli." Isabel swallowed. "I'm so sorry."

"Well. We're both sorry, huh?" He offered a smile, which she returned softly. "But the good news is, once I told somebody—the counselor—how I was feeling, the nightmares started to fade. I try to remember the good parts of my father as I was growing up. I try to realize that God may be up to something in me, making all the bad more than a pointless tragedy."

"How do you...how do you get there?" Isabel's tone was wistful. "I do okay in the daylight, but at night..."

Eli looked upward. *Lord, help me here.* After an imperceptible pause, he sighed. "Patience, I guess. Prayer in every breath. Memorizing Scripture that I can spout back at the devil when he attacks."

"It feels like that, doesn't it?" Isabel said. "An attack."

"Oh, yeah. For me, it was my whole concept of fatherhood on the block. For a while I couldn't trust God because of what my father had done. And I didn't trust myself. Maybe," he added painfully, "maybe I'm still dealing with that."

Isabel stilled, her eyes flashing. "You are a very good man, Eli Carmichael. Don't ever doubt it."

He laughed, pleased at her fierce loyalty. "All right. So noted." He slid one arm under Danilo's legs and lifted him against his chest. "I'm pretty sure it'd take a planetary invasion to wake this kid up. How about showing me where his room is."

Eli slammed the door of the patrol car and settled in with a cup of coffee, ready for a long, uncomfortable vigil. He'd been spending every night when he wasn't working parked down the street from Isabel's house. From this angle he could observe the front, side and unfenced backyard, making sure she and the children were safe.

Owen thought Eli was off the deep end. If Marlon Dean found out what he was doing, he'd be fired, or at the very least put on suspension pending a psychological checkup.

Eli shifted to put his back against the door. Maybe he *was* a bit loony, from lack of sleep. He didn't know how much longer he was going to be able to guard Isabel, look for Bryan Hatcher's killer *and* do his job. He'd managed to snatch a couple hours rest yesterday during lunch, which was going to have to do him for the foreseeable future.

One thing was for sure. He had plenty of time to think. Reaching under the seat, he pulled out his Bible and a flashlight, then sat there in the dark with the sound of Isabel singing to Mercedes playing through his brain. Which made no sense, because Mercedes couldn't hear the music. Maybe she'd been singing for Eli's benefit. He'd gone back to the living room and picked up Isabel's unfinished sampler, then stood there listening.

He'd read the words, "This precious treasure—this light and power that now shine within us," and heard the song at the same time.

He sure didn't *feel* filled with light and power. When Isabel had asked for help, all he could do was sympathize.

He felt loaded up with frustration and weariness.

Wondering how the rest of the passage went, he turned on the flashlight and flipped open the concordance at the back of his Bible. *Treasure.* There it was, 2 Corinthians 4:7.

"This precious treasure—this light and power that now shine within us—is held in perishable containers, that is, in our weak bodies. So everyone can see that our glorious power is from God and is not our own."

A perishable container like a clay pot, that's me. But how was God's power going to be seen in Eli Carmichael's stammering, fragile, everyday life? Rubbing his temples where a headache was growing, Eli closed his eyes and tried to pray.

Lord, I'm wandering around in circles. I've interviewed everybody I can think of, and I can't get Mercedes to talk about the knife.

Mercedes was the key.

Where, Lord? Where did she come from?

Eli had a sudden, vivid image of the first time he'd seen Mercedes. One shoe off, one shoe on, like the old nursery rhyme. If that other little tennis shoe ever turned up, he'd finally get someplace.

Pablo Medieros understood the appeal of a beautiful, well-kept animal. After all, he had grown up on a ranch in Godley, Texas, where he had become equally adept at dodging cow patties and the flat-handed sideswipes of the ranch manager. Tagging along behind his father, who had crossed the border without benefit of immigration papers and hired on to work *Señor* Flaherty's livestock, Pablo had become quite familiar with ranch life.

The bread-and-butter of Flaherty's operation might have been cattle, but in terms of status, the horses clearly reigned. One had to be wealthy to be able to feed and care for, let alone ride and show, a stable full of pure-bred cutting horses. And Pablo had determined, even as a young teenager, that he would one day run his own stable.

He was very close to achieving that dream. The next big run of cocaine across the border would enable him to buy the ranch outside Quemado he'd had his eye on for some months. He would resign his post with the governor, lay down cash for his property and stock it with the finest horseflesh money could buy.

He considered himself a connoisseur, and it was with a mixture of disdain and envy that he strutted through the crowd lining the fence surrounding the main arena at the Eagle Pass stockyard. His purpose at this time was business rather than pleasure.

"Hola, señor," he said as he approached a tall, silver-haired man standing near the gate. Dust swirled in great choking waves, making Pablo wish for a bandanna to cover his mouth and nose. Americans never had the sense to sprinkle the arena before a show in order to settle the dust. Stupid *gringos.*

Rand Hatcher turned, took in Pablo's sport coat, starched western shirt with its bolo tie and eelskin boots. Hatcher's dark brows rose. "'Morning," he drawled. "What can I do for you?"

"Ah, it is more a question of what I can do for *you.*" Pablo smiled and leaned against the fence. "You are pointed out to me as the owner of the champion palomino in the National Cutting Horse Trials. Is this correct?"

Hatcher nodded coolly. "Icharus is mine all right."

He waited without further comment, and Pablo recognized a formidable opponent: a man who refused to volunteer information.

"Then I have a business proposition for you. I am Pablo Medieros, director of security and personal friend of Juan Avila, governor of Coahuila. Governor Avila has charged me with finding a stallion suitable to breed with his prize mare, Music Box Dancer."

"Icharus is not for stud," Hatcher said. "He's a working cutting horse."

"Understood." Pablo removed his Stetson to wipe his perspiring brow. The dust had turned to mud beneath his hat band. "But perhaps our fee will change your mind. The stallion is a most amazing animal, and we are willing to pay well."

"I'll think it over." Hatcher turned away as the roar of a barrel race thundered inside the fence.

Carefully concealed rage flamed between Pablo's eyes. He would not be dismissed like a child. "I trust you will, *señor.* I'll be in touch. Ah, and I almost forget that I am charged by the governor to extend condolences on the recent trouble with your son."

Stiffening, Hatcher fixed Pablo once again with piercing gray eyes. "My son is deceased."

Pablo sighed. "Yes, it is very sad when a boy dies so young in such…tawdry circumstances."

"I don't know what you mean."

"You have put on a brave front, *señor.* Is it not frustrating that one's progeny are not so subject to authority as one's horseflesh?" *Progeny.* Pablo grinned a little, proud of his wide English vocabulary.

"Medieros, what do you want?" Hostility, confusion and distrust radiated from Hatcher's upthrust chin and lowered brows.

Pablo loved being the puppet master of such strong emotions. He began to feel almost benevolent toward his victim. "I do not *want* anything." He shrugged. "I am simply offering to avert disaster from your family name."

Hatcher cast a quick look around. Apparently deciding the conversation was covered by enough noise that it could be continued in the open, he said, "If you don't want me to throw you out of here on your keister, buster, you'd better tell me exactly what you're hinting at. My son was murdered. He didn't do anything illegal."

"It is a good thing I am not easily offended, *señor*," Pablo said silkily. "I will extend grace under these tragic circumstances. Your son most certainly *did* do something illegal, even in our liberal country. He was running drugs."

"You lie!"

Folding his arms against this ridiculous, yes, childish denial, Pablo waited for Hatcher to cede the truth.

After a full, pulsing moment, the gray eyes narrowed in hatred. "Get out of here," Hatcher said through gritted teeth.

"I will leave, *señor,* when you acknowledge the generosity of my offer. I wish to make certain your important friends in the oil industry do not jump to conclusions about your involvement in your son's activities."

Pablo was all admiration. Not one curse word escaped those finely sculpted lips; only a single muscle ticced in the rancher's lean, weathered jaw.

"What do you want?" Hatcher repeated.

"Ah, well, if we are returning favors, then among friends, yes, I would ask a small thing." Pablo stepped closer, but not too close. Americans liked their personal space. "The U.S. Border Patrol has become interested in your son's death. I would like for you to have the investigation called off."

Suspicion darkened Hatcher's gaze. "Why? What do you have to do with it?" He leaned down. "If I find out you were involved with my son's murder—"

"Please." Pablo laughed gently. "Do I look like a man who would soil my hands with violence? No, it is simply that many complex business arrangements will be disturbed if *la migra* sticks its large nose across the border." He studied the turkey feathers in his hat, considering his words. "Clearly it would be in your own best interests as well, to keep them out."

"I'll—see what I can do," Hatcher said jerkily.

"Good." Pablo smiled. "Also there is one other thing if I might continue to beg your indulgence." He replaced the hat on his head. "There is a little girl of about six or seven years, who lived in a bar your son frequented. She has disappeared, and I need to find her. She has no living relatives and would be all alone."

"What would I know about some Mexican street kid?"

Pablo reined in his temper. "I believe your Border Patrol friends have brought her across the border. I merely request that you quietly keep an eye out for this little girl and inform me if you see her. Her name is Mercedes Serraño. I can be reached at this number, day or night." Pablo handed over a business card.

Hatcher reluctantly took the card, stuffed it into his shirt pocket and turned away.

Pablo chuckled and executed a mocking bow to the man's back. *"Hasta luego, señor,"* he said. "Let me know if you decide to breed the stallion."

Chapter Six

In the safety of the big leather recliner, Mercedes and Cindy Lou Who confronted the monster together. Legs slung across one of the chair's arms and head propped against the other, Mercedes had a good view of both *How the Grinch Stole Christmas* and Isabel.

Mercedes had been learning to read English with Dr. Seuss. Entranced by the drawings, she let the rhythm and rhyme of the words fill her head. The wicked Grinch's change of heart opened a world she'd never imagined.

Mercedes glanced over at Isabel. She sat in her rocker, working on her sampler, a pair of tiny, square-lens glasses perched on the end of her nose. Isabel had given her this gift of reading. Showed her in daily, moment-by-moment patience how to connect pictures, thoughts and words.

Mercedes adored Isabel. And not just because she looked exactly like the Madonna that used to hang over

Lupe's bed. Lupe had looked a little like that Madonna, too, but she'd never made chocolate-chip pancakes smeared with peanut butter.

Mercedes had noticed the way Eli looked at Isabel, too, and it made her heart swell to bursting. It was nothing like the hungry, vicious look Pablo had given Lupe.

Mercedes turned a page. She felt safe from Pablo here, especially when Eli was around. Still she often dreamed of Pablo grabbing her heel. Probably his heart was three sizes too small. Maybe four.

If a little girl could fix the Grinch, maybe God could use one to work on Pablo.

Mercedes shuddered. *Please, God, not me.*

Isabel looked up when Mercedes slammed her book shut as if the good Dr. Seuss had suddenly taken to writing ghost stories.

Slipping her glasses into their embroidered case, she put them in her workbasket along with the sampler. She scooped Mercedes into her arms and sat down with her in the recliner. "What's the matter?" she said, making sure Mercedes was watching her lips.

Mercedes shook her head, clutching the book to her chest.

Isabel checked the cover of the book. *How the Grinch Stole Christmas.* She smiled. It was June, barely summer, but children had little concept of seasonal material.

She smoothed a hand over Mercedes's forehead and down her cheek. No apparent fever. *You feel okay?* she signed.

Mercedes nodded, but her brow wrinkled, and she avoided Isabel's eyes.

Right about now Isabel would have given anything for insight into Mercedes's heart and mind. *Lord, You know her thoughts. You know what she's been through. Please help me to help her.*

She'd left the sign language book on the nightstand in her bedroom. Finally, Isabel tapped her temple and slanted her head questioningly.

Mercedes pointed to herself, drew her right index finger along her cheek, then set it beside the left index finger. She turned one palm up, one down, and then flipped them.

Isabel recognized the sign for *sister.* Something about a sister. She took a sharp breath and signed, *What happened to your sister?*

Fat tears began to roll down the dusky-rose cheeks, and Mercedes's mouth trembled. Hiding her face in Isabel's neck, she clung, weeping silently.

Helpless with pity, Isabel held her little girl close, drawing her legs up to create a cocoon of safety and love. How could a hairy green creature in a Santa hat precipitate this sort of grief?

"I love you," she whispered into the top of Mercedes's head.

Eli pushed open the door to *Las Joyas Bellas*—The Beautiful Jewels—an establishment that looked and smelled pretty much like the last three joints in St. Teresa colony he'd visited tonight. Garbage lay in reeking piles in the parking lot, neon beer signs lit the windows, and on the sides of the building, two-foot red letters advertised a popular brand of liquor.

Taking irritated note of some chickens squawking in a slatted crate behind the bar, Eli sat down and, for appearance's sake, ordered a beer. He had no trouble picturing Bryan Hatcher hanging out here. An underachieving twenty-year-old druggie, Bryan had been a trial and embarrassment to his wealthy, churchgoing parents. He'd developed a penchant for crossing the border, where he could satisfy his craving for excitement without getting into trouble with American law. Sad, but not so surprising that he'd been knifed and dumped in the Rio Grande.

Suspecting the kid had been involved in running drugs across his father's property, Eli had been watching him for months. Then Bryan's body had turned up on the American side of the river. But finding the knife on the Mexican side convinced Eli that if he found the killer, he'd also find the smuggling connection.

The biggest frustration was having to depend on Mexican police to investigate on this side of the border. Eli had let them do their thing, but he was tired of waiting. So here he was tonight, unarmed, in civilian dress, definitely not in an official capacity—but determined to at least narrow the possibilities of where Bryan Hatcher had been during his last night alive.

As Eli looked around for the owner of the bar, an enormous man pushed through a beaded curtain at the back of the room.

"Hola, amigo," the man said, docking his immense girth on the stool next to Eli. He gestured toward the barkeeper. "Tequila, *por favor,* Miguel."

Eli nodded. *"¿Qué pasa?"* He continued in Spanish. "This your place?"

The piggy dark eyes squinted even further. "Who wants to know?"

Eli held out a hand. "Name's Dave Jones."

"Señor Jones." The big man shook hands. "I am Hector Caslas. What can I do for you?"

"A friend told me to come here for a good time."

Caslas shook his head, setting rolls of fat jiggling under his chin. "I have very good beer, but that is all."

"But my friend said—" Eli glanced at the barkeeper, who gave him a curious look before busying himself wiping down a glass. "Can we talk privately?"

Caslas's gaze swept Eli's L.L. Bean pullover and Levi's. "Conversation's an expensive item around here."

"I can make it worth your while."

Caslas hesitated, then nodded. "I will at least listen."

Leaving his untouched bottle on the bar, Eli followed Caslas's waddling figure into the other room. The beads clacked and swayed as they passed through. The closetlike little room contained a cot in one corner, a couple of chairs at a cheap plastic table and a bench against the outside wall.

Nothing out of the ordinary.

"Sit down," said Caslas, indicating one of the chairs and depositing his great weight on the bench. It sagged ominously, a fact which seemed not to disturb his genial demeanor. "I assure you we are private. Now what is on your mind?"

"I was hoping you could…hook me up." Eli had no trouble looking nervous. Undercover work had never been his forte, and he could get himself killed. Furthermore, if Caslas wasn't the crook Eli took him to be, he could call the police. Eli's bacon would truly be fried.

"Ah. And what would you like to be hooked up to?" Caslas looked interested.

Bingo.

"I heard you could get good coke down here."

Caslas didn't blink. "Who told you this?"

"My friend. Bryan Hatcher? You know him?"

Caslas pursed his lips and looked at his fat fingers, laced together across his stomach. "I do not have many American customers, and I'm sure I would remember the name. No, I'm sorry. I do not hook up with coke. Only beer." Caslas heaved himself to his feet. "So goodbye, and good look with your search." A wide sweep of his arm indicated that Eli should precede him back through the curtain.

Well, Eli supposed, he should be grateful to escape with his skin and reputation intact. "Thank you, *Señor* Caslas," he said, and reentered the red-lit barroom.

He took another good look around as he left. Something felt unfinished about that conversation, and he was sure Caslas had lied about his ability to supply drugs. That abrupt dismissal at the mention of Bryan's name was telling.

He should send Artemio Petrarca, a Mexican undercover cop with whom he had worked in the past, back over here.

Hopefully Artemio wasn't allergic to chickens.

"Owen! What are you doing here?" Isabel stared at Eli's younger brother, who stood on her porch grinning at her surprise. "And why are you dressed like Jimmy Buffett?" His blond head was covered by a canvas fishing hat, and he had on a pair of wildly flowered swim trunks, a turquoise T-shirt, and flip-flops.

"Eli sent me to rescue the princess." Owen's eyes, the same gemstone color of his T-shirt, glinted with mischief.

Isabel had to admit to a bit of disappointment in seeing Owen, rather than Eli, under that goofy hat. Still, she couldn't help smiling back at him.

"You caught me without my tiara." She looked down at her shorts and bare feet. She'd been up sewing since 7:00 a.m. Bits of thread clung to her red blouse, and she hadn't bothered with makeup. "Do you—um, want to come in?"

Owen shook his head and stepped back. "Nope. I'm just here long enough to hijack your kids and take 'em to the river. Benny's meeting us there with her crew." He tipped his head toward his big diesel extended-cab truck parked on the street. "Be right back. I gotta check the oil." Owen turned, whistling.

"Wait! Eli said not to leave the—" She looked around and lowered her voice when Owen glanced over his shoulder, brows elevated. "Besides, I don't have time to go swimming."

"Oh, you're not going with us." Owen grinned. "Listen, get your two in their swimsuits and pack a couple of towels. Then I'll explain."

Feeling like a drop of water caught up in Hurricane Owen, Isabel scrambled to get Danilo and Mercedes ready. Fortunately, because it was past time to bring Danilo's inflatable pool out of the storage room for the summer, she'd picked up swimsuits for both children the other day at the store. Smiling, she answered Danilo's excited questions while helping him into his trunks, then helped the children gather towels and beach toys.

"I would have figured you for a sports-car man," Isabel teased Owen, walking down the driveway with a child holding each hand. Owen came out from under the hood of his truck, blue-green eyes alight. He wiped the dipstick off and flourished it like a sword. "Been there, done that, crashed it. A long time ago," he added when he saw her face. "I'm a really safe driver now."

Wincing, Isabel boosted the children into the back seat of the cab. "No wonder you're into monster trucks."

"It's just more practical." Owen returned the oil stick, then slammed the hood of the truck. "Eli and I had to have something big enough to haul our horse trailer to the shows."

"I didn't know you had horses." Isabel revised her assumptions about how these two bachelor brothers spent their free time. She knew they went to church and did charity work across the border, but she'd thought…well, what *had* she thought? Barhopping wouldn't suit either of them.

"Technically they belong to our mom. Dad kept a horse for each of us, but now that he's gone—" Owen tilted his head, as if that finished the thought.

Isabel studied him. Compared to Eli, Owen came off as a daredevil who never seemed to worry about anything. Now she wondered.

"Can I ask you something, Owen?" When he nodded, she continued, "Did you have any indication your father was…going off the deep end?"

"You mean like a twitch or something? Fangs?"

"Owen…"

"Just yankin' your chain, sweetheart," he said with a grin.

"How can you be so…so blasé about such a terrible thing?"

"Look, Eli agonizes enough for both of us. I got better things to spend mental energy on."

Isabel noticed he didn't say "emotional energy." She wondered if Owen *had* any emotions. "You didn't answer my question."

He shifted his shoulders again. "I don't think any of us knew Dad that well. He was very contained. Sorta like Eli." He glanced at her. "Which makes me wonder what Big Brother's up to today."

Isabel felt a nervous flutter in her stomach. "What exactly did he say?"

"He just told me to take the kids to the river for the day and he'd be along later to pick you up."

"Pick me up? What for?"

Owen just grinned. "It's a surprise."

"Do you think that's safe? Leaving the house?"

"Just about as safe as it can be. Nobody'll think a thing about two more kids mixed in with Benny's group. She and I'll be there to watch out for them."

"I know they'll have a good time." Isabel shut the door of the truck and leaned in the open window to kiss Mercedes and Danilo, who were bouncing on the seat in excitement. "You two be good, okay?"

"Okay, Mommy." Danilo fastened his seat belt. "Owen, can I dive off your shoulders?"

"You bet." Owen moved around to the driver's seat. "Isabel, I promise I'll take good care of them. Oh, and Eli said to wear comfortable shoes. You're going to be doing some walking."

This is not a date. Isabel stood in front of her closet, absently turning her ring as she tried to figure out what to wear with comfortable shoes.

So very strange, being in her house all alone. Presumably, Fonzie was outside guarding the front porch, but nothing broke the midmorning silence except her own breathing and the sound of the air conditioner.

Me and You, God, she thought. *Now. What do I wear?*

Finally she pulled a short-sleeved cotton blouse off a hanger, then found her denim capris. Eli was going to think she didn't own any other clothes. Which was pretty close to the truth. Oh well.

As she brushed her hair and twisted part of it on top of her head, securing it with an Aztec-style beaded clip, the reflection of her wedding band in the mirror caught her eye. For the first time in six years it looked out of place.

Why? She was a married woman. A Christian widow who had loved her husband. Who *still* loved her husband, she corrected herself with a pang of guilt.

Suddenly it occurred to her that if she walked around with Eli—wherever they were going—with a wedding band on her finger, people would think they were married. To each other. How awkward.

Then she tried to imagine Eli's feelings. Would he be offended or hurt if she left the ring on? Or, despite what he'd said, would he be relieved that she'd left that symbolic wall in place? She'd told him she wasn't ready to think about another relationship.

But was she? She experimentally twisted the ring past the first knuckle, then the second. She laid it on the dresser, felt the nakedness of that third finger. Holding up her hand, she examined the tender skin and had to admit there was no visible indentation. She'd lost weight since Rico died, because she hadn't had much appetite lately, and she probably weighed less than when she got married.

No outward sign of having belonged to Rico Valenzuela. Just one little boy, a house, and a lot of memories.

"Lord, I think this is a good thing," she said aloud. "I feel you smiling at my silliness." Even if she weren't going anywhere with Eli today, removing the ring was right.

Yes, it's time to let Rico go, child, she seemed to hear. *He's here with Me.*

Isabel closed her eyes. "I'll see him again," she whispered.

Feeling as if some solemn, private ceremony had been completed, Isabel picked up the ring and slid it into a drawer where she kept a dried rosebud that had been her prom corsage; her high school diploma, her wedding certificate.

The doorbell rang, and her breath caught.

Eli's here.

Chapter Seven

❧

"Where are we going?"

Eli glanced at Isabel as he backed out of her driveway. He still couldn't quite get over the fact that she sat in the front seat of his car—alone, undistracted by children, dogs, or yard sale items. She didn't really look any different from all the other times he'd seen her. Well, at church she was usually dressed up a little more—skirts and heels sometimes.

But in general she possessed a glowing Latin beauty that drew him in like a de Goya painting.

And she had no idea.

Before he could answer her question, she brushed a hand over her knees and said, "I mean, I didn't have any idea what to wear."

He looked at her again, confused. "Didn't Owen tell you comfortable shoes?"

She laughed. "Yes. Never mind."

"You look great. We're going to Seminole Canyon. Happy birthday."

He was greeted with stunned silence. "How did you know it's my birthday?"

Eli pulled up to a red light and summoned the courage to look at Isabel. He hoped she didn't think he was kidnapping her.

Which, come to think of it, he kind of was.

"I saw the date in the book I borrowed. The Eisenhower biography."

Isabel bit her lip and, to Eli's utter horror, her eyes filled with tears.

"What's the matter?"

She sniffed. "That's the sweetest thing anybody's ever done for me."

"I haven't done anything yet! We're just riding in the car."

"You arranged babysitting and picked me up and surprised me. We don't even have to go anywhere at all now."

"Isabel," he said, shaking his head, "you are hilarious. But please don't sit over there and cry, because the lady in the car next to us is giving me dirty looks."

Isabel gave a watery giggle, then a strangled gasp. "Oh, no!"

"What's the matter now?"

"That's Pamela Hatcher!"

Eli squinted. "Sure is. So what?"

"She's going to think—don't you remember what we talked about the other night?"

Like he was ever going to forget *that* in a million

years. "Oh, yeah." The light changed and he had to concentrate on driving again. "Look, Isabel. I know your concerns, but we'll be back before dark. I promise not to say or do anything that will make you uncomfortable. I'm just your buddy, Eli. Okay?" He glanced at her and found her looking at him, those tears making onyx jewels of her eyes. "I m-mean, it's your birthday. You've been under a load of responsibility for a long time, and you deserve a little downtime."

"Okay." Isabel smiled. "It feels weird, but I think I can do it. And—thank you, Eli. You've been a very good friend to me and Nilo."

Well. That was something, Eli supposed as he took the entrance ramp onto the highway.

He'd thought long and hard about whether or not he should pursue Isabel. During the past five years of living in Del Rio, he'd combed through the single female population until he'd reluctantly concluded God might have marked him for celibacy.

And then, miraculously, like a wildflower in a rocky desert, Isabel's friendship had blossomed out of the tragedy of his father's death.

But while Owen had always been the one with the cavalier attitude who attracted girls liking bad-boy charisma, Eli had no idea how to take a relationship past everyday kindness and courtesy. Flowers? Romantic gestures? The idea made his brain freeze. He suspected he was an emotional coward, a lot like his father.

Now there was a lowering thought.

* * *

Pablo reached the center of the bridge across Seminole Canyon and made the mistake of looking down. His brain whirled like a merry-go-round.

He muttered a curse and crossed himself. Where was a blindfold when you needed one? He'd always been afraid of heights, but the opportunity to follow *la migra* and the beautiful *señora* had been too good to pass up.

He'd almost missed them leaving the house together because Governor Avila had called and asked him to take care of security clearances for a cadre of businessmen from Mexico City. They wanted to cross into Texas for a baseball game in Dallas, and Pablo had to visit the U.S. Immigration office in person to present the authorized papers. Why it could not wait for a more convenient time he did not know.

Clutching the railing, Pablo inched farther across the bridge, keeping his quarry in sight through a thin crowd of tourists. For several days, ever since Rand Hatcher had reported some interesting facts, Pablo had been watching the tall Border Patrol agent called Eli Carmichael. If he'd had any idea the man was such a lover of heights, he would have sent Camino to follow him. As it was, he was having a hard time keeping up.

Ah, at last the end of the bridge. Pablo's breath returned to his lungs where it belonged. He cursed as Carmichael and the *señora* split off from the main body of sightseers, entering a cavern to the left. How was he going to keep an eye on them without alerting them that they were being followed? Their conversation was of great interest to Pablo. He should have worn some kind of disguise.

Then, on the other hand, there was no reason either of them should recognize him. Though his employer often occupied the screen of a TV camera, or the stage of a public forum, Pablo himself might as well have been invisible for all the attention paid a lowly bodyguard.

One day all that would change, of course. Pablo possessed great ambition.

But first he must eliminate that cursed little girl.

Boldly, Pablo followed the agent and the woman into the cave. This man was a very slippery individual. Camino reported that Carmichael, using an assumed name and pretending interest in cocaine, had visited Hector Caslas's place to ask about Bryan Hatcher. Pablo didn't believe for one minute that a good-looking young law officer, particularly one who attended church three out of every seven days of the week, was seriously interested in drugs.

Sidling along, a few feet away from his quarry, Pablo feigned interest in the childlike drawings on the cavern walls. Ignorant savages, what did they know about art? The Spanish *conquistadors* had brought the beauties of fine stained glass and metal work and wood carving into Mexico. Pablo already owned several fine pieces. Soon he would have a place to display them.

The live acoustics in the cavern amplified every word spoken between the man and woman, but unfortunately their conversation concerned children and dogs and church. Pablo's respect for Carmichael diminished rapidly. What man worthy of the name deferred to a woman's interests?

Then Pablo's attention jerked like a metal-detector hitting copper. One of the woman's children was named *Mercedes?* Suddenly the whole thing made sense. Carmichael not only knew where the brat was; he had hidden her with this woman.

Filled with a mixture of anger and satisfaction, Pablo flattened himself against the cavern wall. Where was the girl right now? Was she at home with a babysitter? If he hurried, he might get back there before Carmichael and the woman returned.

He turned, shoved past a couple of tourists entering the cave, and faced the bridge once more. Taking a deep breath to quell his nausea, he focused his gaze on the opposite edge of the canyon. Nothing, not even the dizzying depths of this great hole in the ground, would thwart his purpose this time.

"So you've never been here before?" Eli steadied Isabel with a hand on her elbow as she moved along the uneven floor of Fate Bell Shelter. They'd been examining Native American pictographs along the canyon wall for more than two hours, and he couldn't get over the genuine delight in Isabel's dark eyes. He could tell from the goosebumps on her arms that she was uncomfortably chilly, but she'd wanted to keep going and see as much as possible before lunch.

She gave him a bright grin, pushing her black sunglasses up on her nose. "You know what they say about touring your own backyard. And Rico would rather have had a root canal than spend a day looking at pictures and rocks."

Eli wondered what that said about his own history nerd quotient. "My dad used to bring me and Owen here when we were kids. Good way to burn off that excess testosterone." He followed Isabel to the next drawing.

She wrinkled her nose and pushed the glasses north again. "I can imagine. Nilo will have to get a little bigger, though, before I can bring him out here. He'd give me a heart attack on these cliffs."

Eli turned to follow Isabel's gesture indicating the sweeping sienna and terracotta panorama of boulders, the sheer drop-offs to the Pecos River, and rocky trails zigzagging along the canyon. He smiled. "God's playground."

Isabel wandered over to lean against the guardrail, and Eli followed. Quiet, they stood absorbing the grand, wild starkness of the scene, and Eli remembered something he hadn't thought of in years. "The summer I turned thirteen, Dad took us camping in the Grand Canyon. We had so much junk in our backpacks, I thought we were gonna die before we made it back to the top."

Isabel laughed. "Must be a guy thing. My dad took my brother when he was fourteen."

Eli leaned down to rest his elbows on the top rail and looked over at Isabel. There was so much he wanted to learn about her childhood, her family. "What's your dad like?"

She glanced at him over the top of those slip-sliding glasses. "You'd like him. He's the one who got me interested in history. I think we've visited every fort in the west."

"Is he—are your parents American by birth?"

"No." She smiled. "They were both born in Piedras Negras and immigrated before I was born. My grandparents are still there."

"Really?"

She nodded. "Mama and Daddy started out as migrant fruit pickers. We moved all over the Midwest when I was small, then they made enough money to buy a truck and a little camper. That's what we did our traveling in. Eventually we settled in San Antonio."

Eli tried to imagine Isabel as a bright little Mercedes-like sprite. "So you went to high school there?"

"Yes." She sighed, and somehow he knew she was thinking about her late husband.

He didn't want to open a discussion about Rico. "Where'd you go to college?"

"UT San Antonio, but I barely got started." Eli couldn't interpret her expression, so he waited for her continue. Finally she looked at him. "I'm not very well-educated."

"What are you talking about? You've been jabbering about ancient American history for three hours."

She waved a hand. "Oh, that. That's just what I'm interested in."

Eli nudged her shoulder with his. "Isabel, that's what education is. Studying something you enjoy. Being able to talk about it." He reached up and teasingly removed her sunglasses. "You're either gonna have to get some smaller shades or a bigger nose."

She crossed her eyes. "Can't do much about the nose."

Which was a good thing, Eli thought. It was perfect like it was. He cleared his throat. "Anyway. So if you could go to college again, what would you study?"

"Secondary ed. History." She lifted her chin. "I'm going to go to UTSA when I move back to San'tone. Mama said she'd keep Danilo for me while I'm in class."

Eli had managed to forget all about Isabel's intention of moving. "You could go to college down here somewhere."

She gave him a funny look. "Eli, I have to sell the house in order to afford college. Besides, my family's all in San Antonio. Who'd help me out with babysitting and stuff if I stayed here?"

"Oh, yeah. I guess you're right." Thoroughly unhappy all of a sudden, he looked down. And noticed Isabel's characteristic ring-twisting motion.

Only there was no wedding band on the third finger of her left hand.

As his heart took an acrobatic leap, he tried to think logical thoughts. She'd probably taken the ring off to get it resized. Or she had an infection on that finger.

He was not going to ask her, and he wasn't going to get his hopes up. After all, she'd just told him in no uncertain terms she still planned to leave Del Rio.

But he sure couldn't help wondering.

"Well," he said, "how about lunch and birthday cake? There's a pretty spectacular picnic area not too far from here."

"You brought a *birthday* cake?"

"Well, it's not anything fancy, but yeah, I picked one up on the way over here this morning."

To Eli's astonishment, Isabel reached up and took him by the back of the neck, pulling his head down to her level. She gave him a smacking kiss on the forehead.

"Wh-what was that for?" He felt his face scorch.

"For being so adorable," she said, face alight. "Come on, I'm starving."

Isabel took off for the parking lot, leaving Eli to follow like a man who'd been hit by a bus.

Adorable?

Isabel couldn't wait to get home. Only five more minutes before they pulled into her driveway.

She knew she shouldn't have kissed him. For the rest of the afternoon, every time she'd looked at Eli, he'd flushed scarlet, making those ice-blue eyes, by contrast, a study in panic.

Undoubtedly she'd taken his gesture of friendship entirely the wrong way. She could just bang her head against one of those painted cavern walls for her stupidity.

In total silence they'd finished the sandwiches he'd packed, and gone on to cut thick slabs of gooey chocolate cake without meeting each other's eyes.

How embarrassing. Now what was she going to say to him? There were only so many ways to say thank you without sounding like a fool.

When he stopped the Jeep in front of her house, Isabel grabbed for the door handle. "It looks like Owen's home with the kids." Well, duh. His pickup sat in the driveway.

"I'll just come in and make sure he didn't let 'em tear the house down," Eli said easily. He seemed to have regained some of his composure during the forty-five-minute drive home. "Sit tight for a sec." He got out and loped around to the other side of the vehicle, then he opened her door with a smile.

Isabel blinked. She wasn't used to such small chivalrous acts anymore. She stepped out and looked up at him, feeling the ground shift beneath her feet. He wasn't moving away.

"Eli, thank you again—"

"Isabel, will you stop that?" He sounded mildly impatient. "I've been wanting to take you someplace special for a long time. I told you, you deserve it."

Her eyes widened. Oh. It was about his ridiculous guilty conscience. "The debt's paid," she said stiffly.

He frowned. "I don't know what you're talking about." His eyes narrowed as he studied her face. "Maybe Owen was right."

"Owen? What's he got to do with anything?"

"Not much," he muttered, then took a deep breath as if considering some momentous decision.

Fascinated, confused and suddenly twitchy, Isabel stood under Eli's blue-eyed regard. She needed to get inside the house before the neighbors started wondering what was going on. Mrs. Peterson across the street liked to look out her front window. But something about the way Eli's gaze moved over her face made her stand perfectly still. An intent stare that she recognized in some fundamental way, but couldn't have explained.

"I need to…" she began, and couldn't finish the thought. Eli was leaning down, one hand on the open door, the other on the roof beside her head.

"Close your eyes, Isabel, I'm going to kiss you," he whispered. She obeyed and felt his breath on her cheek, his mouth opening her lips sweetly, and every thought left her head.

Thoughts, she supposed, were highly overrated anyway.

She heard a door slam. Eli jerked away from her, and she remembered she'd been kissing him in broad daylight in front of anybody who happened to be looking out a window or driving down the street.

Or pelting down the driveway.

"Mommy! Mommy! You're back! I dived and Mercedes learned to swim and Owen put a minnow down Benny's back! Can I have an ice-cream sandwich?" Danilo cast himself against Isabel's legs, looking up at her with shining brown eyes.

"I suppose so." Isabel looked around to find Owen himself standing in the front door, holding Mercedes's hand, with a smug smile on his sunburned face.

"I'll take one of those, too," Owen drawled, and she had a feeling he wasn't talking about ice cream.

"Let's—" Isabel gulped "—let me just get in the house and we'll see." She slipped past Eli, who looked as if he'd just walked into a wall. "How did everything go, Owen?" Her lips felt on fire. She wasn't sure she was speaking English.

"Looks like it went pretty well."

She put her hands on her hips. "Owen."

"Well, you asked." He grinned.

"Have you fed them any supper yet?" Isabel marched up the sidewalk, stepping over the dog sprawled across the porch steps. "Hey, Fonzie."

"You mean they have to eat?" Owen said innocently, then called out to his brother. "Come on in, Eli—or haven't you had enough communing with nature for one day?"

Eli gave himself a little shake and shut the passenger door of the Jeep. "I guess I have. Haven't. What are you talking about?" He followed Isabel, swinging Danilo onto his shoulders.

"I just want to make it perfectly clear, yard boy, that you owe me big-time." Winking at Mercedes, Owen stepped aside so that Isabel could enter the house.

She paused in the kitchen doorway, surveying the detritus of a very messy supper spread all over every visible surface. "What exactly have you been doing in here? Dissecting the San Antonio Zoo?"

Owen peered over her shoulder. "They couldn't decide what they wanted, so I gave 'em one of each."

Isabel clenched her hands together to keep from giving Owen a Three Stooges poke in the eyes. "Okay. But popsicles, cheese curls, pretzels and chocolate cookies are not the four basic food groups."

"That explains the black teeth," said Eli from the living room. "And Mercedes looks like she doesn't feel well."

Great, Isabel thought. She was going to pay in spades for her day off.

Chapter Eight

The nightmare came again, this time sending Isabel plunging into darkness. Dark water. Water, drowning suffocating blinding.

She struggled to sit up, wide-eyed and coughing, tears pouring.

Not water. Smoke. Unbreatheable smoke.

Terror poured through her veins as she realized the house must be on fire. She could hear flames crackling from some part of the house.

The children. She had to get to the children—

Scrambling out from under tangled sheets, she slid off the high mattress of her antique bedstead, her feet hitting warm pine. Screaming *"Fire!"* she ran for the open doorway, ducking to find the purest air near the floor. The bathroom night-light shed an eerie glare on the smoke, but she still couldn't see flames.

Prayer mingling with terror, she stumbled into Danilo's room. Yelling his name, she ran to open the window, then snatched her little boy out of his bed. He lay limp in her arms as she leaned out the window and laid him on the ground. *Oh, God wake him up, let him breathe....*

No time to linger. Leaving her precious baby, she crouched back inside the room, where every breath was agony.

Down the hall one more door, her ears roaring and her head beginning to spin. Thank God Mercedes liked the door shut, because it had kept much of the smoke out of the room. In the darkness she found the child's bed, but couldn't wake her. By now Isabel's knees were jelly; she called on her last measure of strength to pick up Mercedes and carry her to the window.

She'd forgotten to open the window first. Bursting into fresh tears, she laid her burden on the floor, then scorched her hand on the lock. She groaned in frustration, caught the hem of her pajama top, and used it to protect her palm as she wrenched open the lock.

After a couple of heaves, she shoved the window up, leaned outside to snatch a quick breath, then lifted Mercedes. Climbing over the windowsill, she slid to the ground and hit her knees.

Air. Fresh, blessed smokeless air.

Thank You, Jesus.

Carrying Mercedes, who lolled like a rag doll in her arms, she struggled through the hedge around the house. She heedlessly trampled the petunias she'd worked so hard to cultivate, hurrying around the corner of the house to reach Danilo's room. There he lay, sprawled in his blue-and-red pajamas, right where she'd left him. Terror froze her brain.

What if she hadn't gotten him and Mercedes out in time?

Suddenly Mercedes jerked and coughed.

"It's okay, baby," Isabel choked out, hugging the little girl. "It's okay, it's okay." Without letting go of Mercedes, she knelt beside her son's inert figure.

Then, slamming against the fear, came rage in a white-hot surge.

"You're not taking him, too!" she screamed, her seared throat aching with blinding pain. Bending over Mercedes's clinging form, Isabel put her mouth to Danilo's, pinching his small nostrils. Rico had made her go through a CPR class a few years ago. She hadn't wanted to, she'd had other things to do that weekend, but oh, how she praised God for her stubborn husband now.

Breathe, Nilo. Please, Lord, let him breathe.

She sat up a little, put her cheek to her son's mouth, and felt nothing. Controlling sobs, she breathed into his mouth again. *Puff, puff, puff.* Wait. *Puff puff puff.*

This time when she sat up, she felt Mercedes turn in her arms. Flinging herself across Danilo's chest, the little girl began to sob in hard, racking spasms.

Isabel was on the point of joining her, when Danilo suddenly heaved, coughed and sucked in air.

Mercedes lit up when she saw Danilo waking and moved off of him, while Isabel grabbed her son into a hug. "Thank You, Lord, oh, thank You!" Over and over she breathed the words, rocking and rejoicing.

She couldn't have said how long she sat there before the burning house registered on her consciousness. Flames had begun to lick toward the roof, pouring out the dormer windows and from the living room onto the porch.

Danilo shoved at Isabel's chest. "Fonzie!" he shrieked, then collapsed in a paroxysm of coughing. "Where's Fonzie?"

"I'm sure he got away, sweetie." She didn't know any such thing, but she wasn't about to go back in that house where the windows were beginning to explode from heat buildup. Isabel got to her feet, holding on to Danilo to keep him from running toward the porch where the dog slept.

The obvious thing to do was to call 911, but she'd left her cell phone in the house. She had no idea what time it was; the sky was a pitch-black blanket, hovering over the smoke and flames devouring her house. The neighborhood slept, oblivious to her distress.

She wavered. Eli lived in an apartment complex a couple of blocks over. The fact that he wasn't in his Jeep parked on the street meant he was working. She would call him, of course, after she got hold of the fire department.

She had to get to a phone.

Grabbing Mercedes's hand, she tugged both children toward old Mr. and Mrs. Peterson's tiny bungalow across the street.

Mrs. Peterson, wearing a woebegone black satin kimono and yellow hair curlers, opened her front door and gaped at Isabel. "What's the matter, dearie?" Then she saw the flames engulfing Isabel's house. "Oh, my!"

Isabel hiccupped. "911—"

"I'll get the phone. Come in." The old lady moved aside to admit Isabel and the children, yelling down the hall, "Howard! Howard, get out here!"

As it turned out, there was little anybody could do, including the Del Rio Fire Department. By the time they arrived, along with the paramedics, the house was a lost cause. Two years ago, Rico had signed on the dotted line, promising Isabel he would turn their property into a showplace worthy of *Better Homes and Gardens*. Now it smoldered in the pre-dawn half-light, a pile of wet, blackened siding, collapsed roofing and shattered glass.

Isabel took one last look at the house as the ambulance screamed away toward the hospital. She sat in the front with the driver, while Danilo and Mercedes lay strapped to gurneys in the back. Her pleas to ride with them had been gently denied. Both children, the lead EMT had assured her, would be fine now that they were on oxygen.

"Tough break," said the driver, a woman, sympathetically. "Husband out of town?"

"No, he's—I'm a single parent," Isabel replied. "I can't believe the smoke alarm didn't go off. I changed the battery just a couple of weeks ago."

"Stuff malfunctions all the time." The driver shrugged. "You'll get a report from the fire marshal, giving you their best guess as to what caused the fire."

Isabel sighed. "At this point I'm just worried about the children." Unbidden tears stung her eyes. She could have lost them both. *Oh, God, what would I do without my babies?* A house could be replaced.

Well, at least I don't have to worry about selling it now, she thought with black humor.

The EMT seemed to have read her mind. "Have you got a place to stay?"

"Well…maybe my neighbors across the street." Mrs. Peterson had offered, but Isabel hadn't committed herself. The Petersons' house was even tinier than her own.

She could drive up to stay with her parents in San Antonio. But there was Mercedes to think of. She'd have to ask Eli what would be best. She'd give anything to lean on him right now.

Which brought to mind the way she'd kissed him yesterday. Unconscionable to encourage a man with whom she had no intention of developing a relationship. She couldn't risk falling in love with another Border Patrol agent. And Eli Carmichael was defined in every way by his job.

Isabel gave the ambulance driver a wobbly smile. "I'm sorry. I can't think straight right now."

"We'll be at the hospital in less than a minute," said the driver. "I'll shut up and leave you alone."

Isabel nodded. She was in desperate need of prayer.

Eli was reading the paper at his mother's breakfast table when his cell phone rang. It was early, only 5:00 a.m., but he had to be at work at six o'clock. Not recognizing the number on the screen, he flipped the phone open. "Carmichael."

"Eli, it's Isabel." Her voice was so hoarse he hardly recognized her.

"Isabel! What's the matter?" She rarely called him, and never this early in the morning.

"I hate to bother you, but I need you to come over to the hospital. There's a problem with—" She huffed a quick breath. "Didn't you hear the fire trucks last night?"

His heartbeat crashed in his ears. "I spent the night at my mom's place." He knew he should have been watching Isabel's house, but her skittish response to their kiss had left him feeling restless. He'd gone over to the ranch to work the horses. "What fire trucks?"

"Eli, my house burned down last night."

"What?" Eli jerked to his feet. His mother, at the stove flipping an omelet, gave him a startled look. "Where are you?"

"I'm in the ER." Her voice wobbled. "We got out before the flames got to the bedrooms, so nobody's burned. But both children are pretty sick from smoke inhalation. I'm okay, just coughing and hoarse…"

Eli closed his eyes. *Lord, thank You they're safe.* "Listen, I'm coming to you. No, I n-need to go by your house and s-see—" He stopped, realizing he was stuttering. His mother had turned off the stove and walked over to put a hand on his arm. "Listen to me, Isabel. Don't call anybody else. Don't answer any questions. I'll be there as fast as I can."

"Okay. Bye." She sounded small and tired. "I'm sorry, Eli."

"Isabel—" But she'd ended the call, so he slapped the phone shut and clipped it to his belt. He was no longer hungry.

He'd *told* her she needed a new fire alarm battery. She should have moved out of that old house a long time ago, sold or not. No way a single woman could keep up with all the maintenance by herself.

Furious, and frustrated that he had nobody to be furious with, he jerked out from under his mother's hand and looked for his keys.

"Eli, what's wrong? Was that Isabel Valenzuela?"

"Yes." He had no desire to explain his relationship with Isabel. "Mom, I've got to go. Thanks for breakfast."

"But you didn't eat anything!"

"I know." He hesitated. "Isabel's house burned down last night. She's at the hospital with the—" He'd almost said "children." He regrouped. "Her son's in bad shape. I need to check on them."

Hands on either side of his face, she held him. "Tell her I'm praying for her," she said softly. "If she needs a place to stay, she can come here."

Eli looked away. His mother had a tender heart, but he couldn't thrust upon her the widow of the man his father had murdered—not like this, anyway, with Mercedes involved.

"Thanks, Mom. You're the best." He grabbed his hat from the rack beside the back door. "I'll let you know."

Isabel had occupied this particular chair in the Val Verde Regional Medical Center ER so many times she was contemplating hanging a plaque above it: The Surrounding Six Square Feet Paid for by the Medical Insurance of Isabel Valenzuela.

She got up to check on Danilo, who lay sound asleep under an oxygen mask, and wished for the umpteenth time she could go home.

But there was no home to go to.

She had called her parents, who were, naturally enough, horrified to hear about the fire. Mom had wanted to come south immediately to pick her and Danilo up, and take them back to San Antonio. It took fifteen minutes to convince her mother she'd be perfectly fine in a hotel room, that she needed to stay here in Del Rio to handle the medical bills and insurance claims and all the other uncertainties that had fallen on her shoulders overnight. She didn't want to think about moving right now.

In fact, Isabel wasn't so sure she wanted to move to San Antonio at all.

Eli needed her. Scratch that—*Mercedes* needed her.

Mercedes lay asleep in the treatment room on the other side of the curtain, and Isabel had worn herself out running back and forth between the two children. Scooting her chair close to the bed, she laid her head down on the sheet next to Danilo's hip.

Let me just close my eyes for a minute....

Sometime later, she felt a light touch on her shoulder. "Isabel? I'm sorry to wake you, but the nurse says the little girl wants you."

Isabel sat up and rubbed her eyes. "Pam! What are you doing here?" Groggily she pulled together the lapels of Howard Peterson's plaid bathrobe, which she'd borrowed to cover her nightgown.

Pam set her handbag on a sink cluttered with medical paraphernalia. "Gracie Peterson called and told me about your house. Oh, honey, I'm so sorry—" She pulled Isabel into a hug. "I want you to come stay with me while you figure out what to do."

Isabel stood stiffly, trying to decide how much to say. Eli would be here any minute, and there was Mercedes on the other side of the curtain. Pam wasn't supposed to know about Mercedes—

Isabel pulled away from her friend's embrace. "Wait here for just a second, okay? Keep an eye on Danilo for me." When Pam nodded, Isabel stepped around the curtain.

Mercedes lay wide-eyed under the bright florescent light, looking small and fragile. Isabel smiled and laid a hand on the pain-puckered brow, smoothing wisps of hair that had escaped from the long black braids.

How do you feel? Isabel signed. At least she thought that was what she signed.

Mercedes tried for a smile, but touched her throat. Her eyes teared up.

Isabel wanted to take the little girl's pain on herself. The best she could do was lean down and lay her cheek against Mercedes's. She felt the child relax.

"Jesus, ease her pain and help her sleep," Isabel whispered.

"Mrs. Valenzuela?"

Isabel turned her head to find the ER nurse in the doorway. "Yes?"

"The doctor wants to admit all three of you for the rest of the day, to make sure oxygen perfusion goes back to normal. He may keep you through the night. The children have breathed in enormous amounts of carbon monoxide." The nurse paused, an awkward expression on her round face. "Have you been able to confirm that insurance information we asked for on the little girl? And we've got to locate her previous medical history somehow."

Isabel stood up, leaving her hand on Mercedes's shoulder. "I told you, this is kind of a delicate situation." She kept her voice low, hoping it wouldn't carry to the other side of the curtain. "Agent Carmichael should be here any minute—"

"Here I am, Isabel. What's going on?"

At the sight of Eli's clean-shaven, sun-browned face, Isabel nearly broke down in fresh tears. Her emotions were way too close to the surface.

Blinking hard, she pulled in a deep breath. "It's just that we don't have any medical records for Mercedes. I don't know what she's allergic to, what inoculations she's had—"

Eli smiled down at the nurse, who blushed as if she were fifteen instead of at least twice Eli's age. "Jeri and I have a longstanding relationship, don't we? Let's go get this straightened out right now." He looked at Isabel, calmness and confidence radiating from his blue gaze straight to her heart. "Don't go anywhere, I'll be right back."

Eli and the nurse had barely vacated the doorway when the curtain skated back on its rod, and Pamela poked her head around. "Was that Eli Carmichael?" she asked. "What's he doing here?"

"The same thing you are," Isabel said. "Checking on us."

"He's certainly been the attentive suitor lately. That was you I saw the other day at the red light, wasn't it? Why were you crying?"

Isabel felt like a specimen under a microscope, though she was certain her friend hadn't intended to put her on the spot. Her face must have shown her unease, for Pamela put a well-manicured finger across her lips.

"Okay, I'll leave you alone. You've got enough to worry about." Her glance brushed over Mercedes. "Who *is* this little girl, anyway?"

Currently operating on little more than emotion and rapidly draining adrenaline, Isabel blurted, "This is Mercedes." She reached out and took Mercedes's small hand. "She's staying with me for a little while."

"Really." Pamela approached the foot of the bed and smiled at Mercedes. "I wondered what you were doing with a girl's swimsuit in your shopping cart the other day! Isn't she beautiful? Is she your niece? How old are you, darling?"

"She doesn't hear or speak," Isabel said as Mercedes faintly squeezed her hand. "She's seven." *We think.* Unwilling to flat-out lie, she ignored Pamela's question about her relationship to the child.

Pamela clasped her hands together. "Then of course she comes with you to my house. When will you be released?"

"Tonight at the earliest. Probably tomorrow." Isabel reached for her rings, then realized she'd never gotten around to putting them back on. They were in that dresser drawer—burned up, along with every other item that meant anything to her. Pictures. Clothes. Keepsakes. Even that stupid bowling ball. She wanted to burst into tears, but what good would that do? The verse about storing up treasures in Heaven suddenly rang in her head with bell-like clarity.

"Bless your heart," said Pamela, with true southwestern sympathy. "Tell you what, I'll go shopping and buy you a couple of new outfits. That'll make us both feel better. What are you, about a size six?"

"Um, I don't think so—"

"Yes, and definitely petite." Pam whisked back around the curtain to retrieve her bag. She reappeared, resolved in her self-appointed mission. "Since Eli's here to look after you, I'll take care of clothes for the children, too, and freshen up the guest rooms." She kissed Isabel's cheek and marched toward the door. "Don't worry about a thing."

Worry? Isabel collapsed into the chair beside Mercedes. What did she have to worry about?

Chapter Nine

Eli knew he was a goner when Isabel—even dressed in a '70s-era bathrobe and smelling like an ashtray—could make his tongue fall out of his head. He loved the sleepy eyelids veiling those magnetic dark eyes, the blue-black sheen of her hair, and the tiny beauty mark above the corner of her mouth. He loved her laugh and even the sparkle of tears when she got emotional. He loved the way she fit just under his shoulder when he walked beside her.

He was definitely doing a tango with the L word. However, she *was* going to explain to him why she'd agreed to stay with Pamela Hatcher.

The pediatric ward at suppertime was a zoo: crying babies, nurses hollering for back-up, carts rattling past loaded with metal trays. And the smells…

Eli longed for the relative peace of a good shoot-out.

"So Pam thinks Mercedes is your niece?" He peeled the top off a container of Jell-O and handed it to Mercedes. She beamed at him and began to eat as if it were her last meal on the way to the gallows.

"I think so. I didn't correct her anyway." Isabel stood beside Danilo, watching to make sure he didn't spill milk all over his hospital gown. They'd already changed his sheets twice.

"I'm impressed, Mrs. Valenzuela. Didn't think you had it in you." Eli sat down in a visitor's chair.

Isabel gave him a look. "I am not comfortable with lying to my friend. How can she pray for me if I don't tell her—"

"Mom," said Danilo around his straw. "A superhero can't reveal his identity, remember?"

Eli grinned. If the small-fry got it, surely he could depend on Isabel's discretion. He relaxed as much as possible in the uncomfortable chair. "I've arranged a safehouse for you and the kids. It'll be ready in a day or two."

Isabel's eyes flashed. "I don't see why that's necessary. There hasn't been one sign that anybody's actually looking for Mercedes."

"Can we look for Fonzie before we go to the safety house?" Danilo was looking at his mother, wide-eyed at her vehemence.

Eli sighed. "We'll do our best to find him." He picked up the TV remote and found a cartoon station. "Here, squirt, finish your milk and watch your cartoons."

Isabel accompanied him, her reluctant expression making it clear she didn't want any more bad news. He turned her to face the window and stood behind her, hands on her shoulders. He bent close to her ear. Whew, she stunk of smoke. He smiled in spite of his worry.

"Okay, here's the deal," he said, and felt her shiver. "The fire was no accident. I walked through your house with the fire marshal. He hasn't had time to file the report yet, but there was evidence of arson."

Isabel had stiffened more with each word until her back shook against his chest. For propriety's sake he'd left the door wide open. He knew it wouldn't look right if he pulled her into his embrace.

So he tightened his clasp on her shoulders and softened his voice. "I don't know how they found out where Mercedes is, but we can't take any more chances. Y'all can go home with Pam tomorrow, but the three of you are disappearing as soon as I can arrange—"

"Somebody deliberately burned down my house? Tried to kill us?" Isabel's voice was a horrified whisper. She had crossed her arms across her stomach, a protective gesture that went to his heart.

Eli could see the edge of her profile, the tremble of her lips. He had no words to comfort her or relieve her fear. "I'm so sorry," he said. "I should have never gotten you into this mess. If I'd been there last night—"

"You might be dead," she said fiercely. "Don't be stupid, Eli, it was my choice to do this. And we can't change what happened. I'm sad about losing my stuff, but—stuff is *stuff*. I'll do whatever I have to, to keep my children safe."

Eli wondered if she realized she had claimed Mercedes as her own. "You're a trooper." He released her shoulders.

"No." Isabel whirled to face him. "I am not a trooper, I'm a homemaker and a mom. I agreed to help you because that little girl needs somebody to love her, but I will not let Border Patrol run my life indefinitely. If you don't catch the bad guys within about forty-eight hours, I'm moving to San Antonio where it's safe for me and my kids." She notched up her chin. "Do you hear me?"

He whistled at her vehemence. "I hear you." He heard her words, and he also got the subtext. She wouldn't be kissing any more Border Patrol agents in the future. "But I can't make any guarantees about how long this will take."

"Well, just so you know how I feel." She stuck her hands in the pockets of that ugly bathrobe, stepped around him, and walked over to check on Danilo.

Unfortunately, Eli knew exactly how she felt.

The Hatchers' ranch house—which, in Isabel's mind, qualified as a mansion—backed up to a man-made lake stocked with catfish and landscaped with flowering shrubs. The estate included a thousand acres on the Rio Grande, the main source of water for the ranch.

Yawning, Isabel shifted in her poolside chaise longue. The splash of the waterfall should have lulled her right to sleep. Luxurious to be clean and dressed in comfortable clothes, but she couldn't shake a feeling of restlessness.

"You look so tired. Why don't you go on up to bed?" suggested Pamela, who floated nearby on a raft. "Rand and I will keep an eye on the kids."

Isabel shook her head. "I'm too keyed up to sleep." A ripple of childish giggles caught her attention. Through the wrought-iron fence she could see Rand Hatcher helping Mercedes and Danilo feed the fish. Every fistful of bread crumbs brought a noisy churning to the surface of the water.

"Mercedes is a sweet little thing," Pam observed with a sigh. "Rand and I were looking forward to having grandchildren one day. But now…" Her voice petered out in sadness. "Well, now, of course, that will never happen."

Isabel wondered what Pamela would do if she knew Mercedes had probably witnessed her son's murder.

"How did you get through it?" Pamela had hooked the heel of one foot across the edge of the pool so that she could talk to Isabel without floating away. "How did you keep bitterness from eating you alive when that monster killed your husband?"

That monster was Eli's father. Getting to know Eli and Owen, appreciating the depth of their shame, had lessened Isabel's rage, if not her sense of loss. She shrugged, uncomfortable with giving spiritual counsel to her older friend.

"I did what you've always told me to do. Prayed a lot. Cried out to God. Read from the Psalms." Laying her head back against the chair, Isabel watched a flock of ducks paddle across the lake. "Frankly I've been so busy keeping Danilo out of trouble and trying to make ends meet, I haven't had time to dwell on myself."

Pamela dabbled her hands in the water. "I read my

Bible every day. It says to forgive. But how can I, when I don't know who did it or why?"

"I went for a whole year without knowing. If Rico's partner hadn't made it his mission to figure it out, I might still be in the dark." She hesitated. "I think sometimes God leaves us in the dark to force us to trust Him."

"Boy, that's depressing."

Isabel smiled. "Maybe it seems that way. But what if we choose to believe God's going to do something miraculous, in spite of the way things look?" She heard her own voice growing more confident as she spoke. "What if we believe God really is…you know—*for* us?"

Pamela stared at Isabel for a moment, expression blank. Finally she pushed away from the side of the pool. "Well, it would truly be miraculous if anything good came out of this whole mess."

If she looked at the situation from a worldly point of view, Isabel would have to agree. She couldn't even go to her house to go through the ruins looking for keepsakes, because Eli had forbidden her to leave the Hatchers'. She had no idea if anything remained after the fire.

She closed her eyes and listened to the soft evening sounds of the waterfall and the katydids singing in the shrubbery.

Lord, I know You've heard my cry for help. Please show Pam how much You love her, too.

Artemio Petrarca was a wiry young Mexican cop who could blend into just about any setting without raising an eyebrow. Eli picked him up at the Mexican checkpoint on the international bridge, then turned to drive back onto U.S. soil. No matter what Marlon Dean thought, it was past time to compare notes.

Temio slouched in the passenger seat of Eli's Border Patrol SUV without bothering with a seat belt. American law didn't impress him much. He pointed the air conditioner vents at his face and turned the fan knob to full blast. "Man, some days I'd kill for an hour in a walk-in freezer."

Eli smiled. "We'll stop by KFC and ask for a tour, if you want."

Temio just grinned. "So, what's the lowdown, my brother?" he drawled. Temio loved to practice his English, but sometimes he sounded like a character from a bad cop show.

"The situation's escalated over here," Eli said. "Somebody burned down Isabel Valenzuela's house night before last."

"You're joking."

Eli shook his head grimly. "I wish. Somehow, somebody knew my witness was there."

Artemio was silent for a moment. "I haven't said a word about her to anybody."

"I know you wouldn't." Eli hesitated. "My supervisor was the only person besides me and my brother who knew where she was. Dean's got it in for me."

Artemio whistled. "So what are you gonna do?"

"I don't know yet." Eli choked on disgust every time he pictured Dean double-crossing him. "Did you get a chance to check up on Hector Caslas?"

"Yeah. Seems to be just your garden variety pimp."

Eli put that information in context of that dark, rat-infested storeroom where he'd talked with Caslas. "Something about his place wasn't right. The way he shut me down when I mentioned the Hatcher kid."

"Look, man, I been keeping my ear to the ground, like you asked me to. Hatcher was pretty well-known in the bars. Had a thing for Mexican hookers."

"The fast track to slow death," Eli said, parking in front of a convenience store just off the bridge. "Come on, I'll buy you a Coke."

The two men entered the store, where the female clerk appreciatively eyed Eli's uniform and dismissed Artemio with a glance. Eli paid for the drinks, stood back and watched his friend flirt with unquenchable Latin hubris. By the time they left, Temio had the clerk's phone number in his pocket. Owen could take lessons.

Smiling, Eli started the car and pulled out of the parking lot. "So. Any names connected to Hatcher's love life?"

"Yeah, but I suspect it's a stage name. They call her Diamond. She's disappeared, though. Nobody's seen her since the night Hatcher was killed. Some say she might have done it herself."

"That's something." Eli downed half his soft drink as he thought about it. "Maybe you could keep digging. Find out her real name."

"You know I'll do what I can, man."

"I appreciate it. Listen—"

Headlights in the rear-view mirror caught his attention. An old, boxy van was following too close. He'd pull the guy over and give him a ticket if he didn't have so much else to think about.

He glanced at Artemio. "I'd better take you back. I've got to get back to the Hatcher's place and keep an eye on—" Eli broke off as the truck lurched, nearly jerking the steering wheel out of his hands. The van behind him had hit him from the rear.

Bracing himself against the dash, Temio broke into a string of colorful Spanish as Eli got control of the wheel. "What's that fool doing?"

"He rammed me on purpose," said Eli, swinging into the opposite lane to avoid another collision. He braked, letting the van skid past, and picked up the radio. He memorized the tag number and read it to the dispatcher, along with his location. "Backup requested," he finished, and took off after the van. "You might want to fasten your seat belt," he told Artemio.

Despite the vehicle's apparent age, the driver of the van manipulated the Del Rio streets with remarkable speed and agility. Eli chased him for a mile or so before he heard the wail of a siren approaching from the north. Backup at last.

But before he could blink, the van suddenly screeched into a U-turn, emitting the *pop-pop* of gunfire. Eli instinctively jerked the wheel, Artemio roared, and the SUV hit the hard shoulder.

Everything went tumbling.

Holding a tiny orange-striped kitten under her chin, Mercedes peeked over the stall door. She couldn't see

Danilo now, but a few minutes ago he had run out of the barn into the dark. They were playing *el bote*—the tin can—similar to *escondidas,* the hide-and-seek game she'd learned in the streets of St. Teresa. *Señor* Hatcher had brought them out here after supper to see the kittens and to give Isabel time to talk to her friend, the *señora.* Isabel had told Danilo not to leave the barn. Mercedes wondered if she should tell on him.

Danilo was sweet, but so silly. Using a mixture of Spanish and English and goofy made-up hand signs, he'd insisted on being "it." Then, in order to make the game fair, he'd stuffed his ears with wads of cotton he'd brought from the bathroom. She'd laughed at him, but agreeably kicked his empty soup can all the way to the other end of the barn.

While Danilo chased the can, Mercedes had slipped into the stall to hide. She hadn't been able to resist another look at the kittens, sleeping in a furry, squirmy heap next to their mama. When after a long time Danilo still hadn't found her, she had decided to look out. That was when she'd seen him leave the barn.

Now she wondered where *Señor* Hatcher was. She had last seen him going into a tack room with a tiny cell phone pressed to his ear. She felt the kitten vibrating against her neck and rubbed her cheek against the top of its head for comfort. There was nothing to be afraid of exactly, but she didn't like being left all alone.

She decided to give up, and if Danilo saw her before she got to bang the can on the ground, well—so, she lost. Not so big a deal. Returning the kitten to his brothers and sisters, she opened the stall door, then walked boldly down the center aisle of the barn. She looked with interest at the beautiful horses *Señor* Hatcher kept. Big, sleek animals with bright eyes and well-brushed manes, they thrust their noses over the doors as she passed. They didn't frighten her as long as they stayed in the stalls.

Where was Danilo? It was almost a let-down to simply pick up the red-and-white can, smack it against the concrete floor, and know that she'd won the game.

There was the tack room. She tried the door and found it locked. Alarm bumped under her ribs. She wondered if she could find her way back to the house in the dark alone.

Isabel jerked awake at a knock on the guest bedroom door. She looked at the clock and saw with a start that it was nearly nine o'clock. She'd been so tired after supper that she'd taken Rand up on his offer of entertaining the children, and promptly fallen asleep. She should have had Danilo and Mercedes in the bathtub long ago.

She jerked open the door. "Pam! I'm sorry, I didn't mean to sleep so long, I hope the kids haven't—" Then Pamela's stricken expression registered. "What's the matter?"

"Oh, Isabel," Pamela burst out, "we've looked everywhere for him."

"What?" Isabel's stomach dropped. "Are you talking about Danilo?"

"Yes! I'm sorry, I'm so—" Pamela's voice broke. "I can't even think. We've been looking for him for the last half hour, and I guess we need your help. I could just strangle Rand, he was supposed to be watching them, but he got a phone call—"

"How long has he been gone?"

"We—we don't know exactly. Rand had them out in the barn looking at a new litter of kittens. He says they were playing a game, and one minute they were both right there, the next they weren't."

Isabel wanted to scream with fear. "You mean Mercedes is missing, too?"

"No, she's right downstairs. She walked all the way back to the house by herself in the dark, so I called Rand to find out what happened to him and Danilo." Pamela's voice shook as she continued. "I didn't want to wake you if it was, you know, a false alarm, so I took Mercedes with me and drove back to the barn to help look for Danilo."

"And you didn't find him," Isabel said stupidly. *Oh, Lord in heaven, my little boy! Not my little one.* "Okay, call the police right now, while I talk to Mercedes." She stopped. Eli should know about this before she did anything else. "Wait." She sucked in a lungful of air. *Calm down.* "Pamela, don't do anything until I call Eli. Have Rand keep looking, though."

"All right." Pamela sounded doubtful of Isabel's sanity.

Isabel knew she sounded crazy, and she *felt* out of control. Shaking, she dialed Eli's cell phone number.

Flailing legs kicked Pablo's knees as he ran across the pasture with his hand clapped across the child's mouth. He knew he only had a few moments to get his victim to the car and away from here.

After following the Valenzuela woman and the two children from the hospital, he and his men had been forced to skulk around the perimeter of the estate. Rand Hatcher would not deign to return his calls. But after several hours of watching the house through binoculars, he'd finally seen the rancher take the two children to the barn. Realizing it might be his only opportunity to get near the girl, he'd followed.

Now, running full-tilt, he called on every ounce of the strict conditioning with which he maintained his body. After all that waiting, it had been ridiculously easy to snatch her as she ran around the barn straight into his arms. He planned how he would grab the rope and duct tape out of the trunk, tie her up, and leave her there for the trip across the border.

When he reached his car, Pablo took his hand off the child's mouth long enough to reach for his car keys. That was when he discovered his mistake.

The child in his arms let out a bloodcurdling scream. "I'm gonna get you, you villain!"

Pablo found the presence of mind to clap his hand over the boy's mouth, even as white-hot rage all but blinded him. Incoherent thoughts swirled as he completed, by rote, the actions he'd planned to restrain his captive. It had been dark, he excused himself. The child's silence had led him to believe it was the mute little girl. The two children were nearly the same size.

Staring down at the boy, now lying in the trunk with

his hands and feet tied, duct tape firmly strapped across the lower part of his face, Pablo could hear him sniffling, a pathetic sound which bothered him not one whit. He slammed the lid of the trunk.

He had to get away from here. It would be all right. He would simply trade the boy for the girl. What mother would refuse to trade a street urchin for her own flesh and blood?

Chapter Ten

Eli woke up groaning. He was going to throw that cell phone into the river next chance he got. He turned his head, trying to find a more comfortable place on the pillow.

Jagged-edged pain nearly split him in two.

"Carmichael. Come on, we gotta get you out of here before this thing blows up."

"Temio?" Eli winced at the sound of his own voice. Artemio had the door of the SUV open, trying to disengage Eli's seat belt. Trouble was, he was upside down and bleeding like a pig in a butcher shop window. "What happened? You all right?" At least the phone had quit ringing.

"Yeah. Air bag caught me."

After one more brain-jarring yank, Eli fell out of the vehicle into Artemio's arms and he passed out again.

Sometime later he woke up again with paramedics crawling all over him. "Temio?" he croaked.

"Right here, man," said Petrarca from somewhere behind the crowd of EMTs. "You been making enemies while I wasn't looking. Better cool your jets for a while."

"Did they catch the guy who hit us?"

"Abandoned his car. We lost him."

"What about the car? Registration?"

"Stolen," Artemio said shortly. "Would you shut up and let the police worry about it? There's a pretty good sized goose egg on your head, man."

"Lie still, Agent Carmichael," said an exasperated paramedic. "We're going to load you up and take you to the hospital."

"No, you're not!"

"Carmichael, I promise I'll check on Isabel," said Artemio.

"Where's my phone? It was ringing a minute ago." Eli felt himself being lifted. He was strapped to the gurney like a mummy. "Wait!" he shouted. Only it came out like a doggone whisper. "I'm not going anywhere until I know who was calling—"

"All right, hold up, guys," said Artemio. "Let me just check his phone before you take him." Eli could hear him muttering about being an answering service. After a moment he said in surprise, "It was Isabel."

With a supreme effort Eli opened his eyes and glared at the EMT at the foot of the gurney. "If you don't let me off this thing *right now* and give me my phone, I'm gonna make sure you're fired."

The EMT, about two hundred pounds of solid muscle, laughed. "Yeah, and I'll be a lot more likely to get fired if I *do* unstrap you. Knock it off, dude, you're off to the ER."

"Artemio, call her" was all Eli had time to say before they slid him into the back of the ambulance and slammed the doors.

All the way to the hospital, he worried, prayed, and gritted his teeth to keep from throwing up. Artemio was right about one thing. Eli had made somebody angry enough to try to kill him outright. Which meant that Isabel and Mercedes were in the crosshairs, too.

By the time he'd been examined by a harried young ER doc and shot full of enough antibiotics to ward off the bubonic plague, Eli was ready to deck somebody. Then his brother ambled into the room dressed in dusty denims.

"Where have you been?" Eli snarled.

"Working the horses. Unlike some people, I have a life." Owen removed his hat and bumped the dust off against his leg. "Hear you had a tough day."

"Where's Artemio? Has anybody called Isabel yet?"

"Well aren't you the romantic hero?" Owen grinned. "Don't think she'd be too impressed with your looks at the moment."

Eli glared at his brother. "I'm feeling much better thanks. And if they don't unplug me from this IV in about ten seconds, I'm going to do it myself. Go get the nurse."

Owen whistled. "Okay, this would be a good time to breathe. The nurse it is."

He was back in a moment with the RN, who gave

Owen a disapproving sniff and marched over to unhook Eli's drip. "The doctor says you can go now."

"Is Artemio Petrarca around?" Eli asked the nurse.

"The little guy with the cell phone? I threw him out thirty minutes ago." The nurse picked up Eli's wrist to feel for his pulse.

"Threw him out?" Eli yelped.

"He's standing out under the canopy smoking," said Owen.

"Well, go—"

"—get him," Owen finished with Eli. "Why didn't you say so when I went out the first time?"

"No cell phones in here," the nurse informed Eli. "Interferes with the equipment."

"No problem, I'm leaving." Eli sat up to button his shirt.

"Just make sure you change the dressing on that cut on your head tomorrow. It should heal in a couple of days." The nurse fixed Eli with a minatory stare. "No driving tonight."

Owen came in just then with Artemio in tow. "I'll keep him out of trouble," Owen said.

Artemio tossed Eli his cell phone, tacitly daring the nurse to object. "I talked to Isabel," he said, and cleared his throat. "Bad news, man. Her boy's missing."

Isabel had to get out of the house, away from Pamela's concern and guilt. She walked out onto the deck, avoiding the lighted pool area in favor of the shadows of the yard. Opening the gate, she stepped down off the deck and headed for the grassy area between the pool and the lake.

Danilo still hadn't turned up.

And according to Artemio Petrarca, Eli was in the hospital after someone had run him off the road.

Crazy. I'm crazy, Lord. I'm so angry and upset and...

She bowed her head. "I don't know what to do," she said out loud. Somehow she felt better, admitting her weakness and confusion. "I thought it was over when Rico died. I thought nothing else bad would happen to me for the rest of my life. Didn't you say death is the big sting?"

No. She remembered now. The Word said, "Death, where is your sting?" In Christ, death lost its power.

It was getting through *life* that put you in the crucible.

Isabel fell to her knees in the grass and pressed her hands to her face. "Oh, God, where's my baby?" she groaned. She couldn't even cry, had no tears left. Dropping her hands, she looked up at the moon smiling down, silent and calm.

Where was God?

She didn't know how long she'd been sitting there when she felt a small hand on her head. With a thrilling start of hope, she looked around for Danilo.

Mercedes stood there, the warm, dry night breeze blowing her long black hair around.

I'm scared, she signed. *Where's Danilo?*

Isabel stifled her own pain and pulled the little girl into her lap, hugging her tightly. "I don't know," she whispered, even though Mercedes couldn't hear the words.

Mercedes pulled back and pressed her palms together. *Prayer.*

"Yes. I'm praying." Isabel enfolded Mercedes's small hands in hers. What else could she do? "Lord, I feel so weak. I want to believe You'll bring Danilo back to me. I don't want to be afraid."

She thought about Eli's suggestion of "spouting Scripture." If she'd ever been under attack it was now. Somehow, though, she couldn't think of a single Bible verse.

At four o'clock in the morning, Eli found Isabel sound asleep on the Hatchers' living room sofa, the phone tucked under her cheek. Pamela had let him in, then retired to the kitchen to make coffee.

He woke Isabel gently, but she jerked upright as if she'd been having nightmares.

"Eli! Did you find him?"

Eli rubbed his thumb against the button impressions on her face. "No. Owen and I have been looking all night." He sat down beside her and laid his head back against the sofa.

"You look awful." He could feel her shifting closer, then her fingers brushed the edges of the bandage on his head. He wished he could lay his aching head in her lap and sleep for a year.

"Feel pretty rough." He opened his eyes and found her close enough to kiss. Isabel in the morning. Pam had better get back in a hurry.

Then Isabel said, "You shouldn't be here."

Cold water indeed. He sat up and rubbed his eyes. "I came to see if you'd heard anything on Danilo."

"We haven't," said Pamela, coming back in with

three steaming mugs on a tray. Looking troubled, she offered the coffee to Isabel and Eli. "Rand thinks he may have just wandered off. There's all kind of predators around here. Or he could have fallen into the lake."

Eli noticed Isabel's sudden pallor. "Pamela," he said warningly, and looked around. "Is Rand still in bed?"

Pam frowned. "No. He left shortly after midnight. He knows people in the police department. I think he hoped he could speed things up."

Something about that struck Eli as odd, but he couldn't put his finger on just what. "Every search-and-rescue team in the county's on it."

Pamela sniffed. "Forgive me if I don't have a lot of faith in our local police. Or the Border Patrol."

"They're doing the best they can." Isabel laid her hand on Eli's wrist, and he glanced at her in surprise. Her eyes looked bruised, but there was a light in them that made him admire her courage all over again. "They'll find him."

He hoped her confidence wasn't misplaced. "Listen, the other reason I came by was to let you know we're putting you under twenty-four-hour police protection. They're sending over a woman who's experienced in hostage situations."

"Do you really think that's necessary?" asked Pamela.

Eli just looked at her, then turned to Isabel. "I've got to go. Will you walk me to the door?"

She nodded and set her mug on the coffee table.

When they reached the front door, he looked down at her for a moment. "I take full responsibility for this," he said quietly. "I thought you'd be safe enough here but—"

"Eli—"

"But I *will* get him back." He reached in his pocket and showed her a tiny cell phone. "I want you to call me if you hear anything from a kidnapper. Tell Officer Beatty, of course, but—" He picked up Isabel's hand and laid the phone in her palm. "Call me no matter what time it is. And keep Mercedes close."

Isabel swallowed. "I will. What are you going to do?"

"Interview a couple of informants. Check in at the station." Reluctantly he opened the door. He wished he had the right to tell her he loved her. "Get some sleep, okay?"

Isabel uttered a humorless laugh. "I'll try."

He heard the lock click behind him as he left.

Isabel spent the hour after Eli left on her knees beside her bed. She prayed for Danilo's safety. She prayed for Eli and the police to have wisdom. She prayed for her own strength of mind and spirit. Peace seemed like some foreign language, one she'd heard about but only vaguely understood. The phone rang a couple of times, and each time Isabel nearly jumped out of her skin.

The third time it shrilled, she didn't look up until the door opened. Pamela stood in the doorway with a cordless phone clutched to her chest. "Isabel, it's for you."

"For me?" Isabel felt like the victim of a fever-inducing infection. Her eyes ached from crying, her forehead felt tight, and her body moved sluggishly as she got to her feet. "Who is it?"

"I don't know." Pamela looked apprehensive. "He wouldn't identify himself." She handed the phone to Isabel and backed away reluctantly. "Let me know if I can do anything."

"Thanks." Isabel waited until Pamela had closed the door again before she put the receiver to her ear. "Hello?"

"Mrs. Valenzuela? I have your little boy."

Isabel sat down hard on the bed. The deep voice was electronically distorted, unrecognizable. "Who is this?" she whispered.

The caller did not answer her question. "Give me the deaf girl, and you can have the boy back," he said. "Keep everybody else out of it or he dies."

Isabel's vision blurred. "I can't get out of the house. They're sending a guard."

"I will call again at midnight with final instructions. If you tell anyone you talked to me, I will know, and I will kill your son."

Isabel was incapable of answering.

"Mrs. Valenzuela, do you understand?"

"Yes," she made herself say.

"Good. Do you have a cell phone?"

She had the one Eli had given her this morning. Cruel irony that she had to use it for this purpose. "Yes, I have one."

"Put it on vibrate mode so that you will awaken no one when I call. Go into a closet to answer. What is the number?"

"Just a minute." Isabel fumbled to look up the unfamiliar number and read it to the hateful person on the end of the line.

"Good. Remember, midnight. Nobody is to know." The phone clicked in her ear, followed by a dial tone.

Isabel squeezed the phone in numb hands and sank to her knees beside the bed. Nobody could help her. Rico was dead. Eli unavailable. Even God seemed very far away.

Mercedes stood in the bedroom doorway, watching Isabel on her knees praying.

She wished she could get rid of Isabel's worry and sadness. Danilo was such a baby, always getting in trouble. He didn't know how good he had it. If Mercedes had a mother like Isabel, she'd never do *anything* wrong.

She'd crept down the stairs this morning and watched Eli talking to Isabel. He'd had that *look* on his face, like a knight in one of the fairy tales her teacher had read to the class last year. Americans were always bringing junk across the border and leaving it for people to pick through. Sometimes there were beautiful things like that old book. The cover had fallen off, but the pictures…

Mercedes had pored over those pictures every time she could get away with it, and she had even copied some into her tablet. Ladies with long golden hair, princes with flowing capes—even the wicked witches and ogres had captured her imagination and made her hungry for paints like those used by the artists.

Isabel understood that hunger and let her draw whenever she felt like it. Isabel praised her pictures, and seemed amazed that such a poor little girl could produce them.

Well, sometimes even Mercedes herself was surprised by what appeared on the paper. And frightened.

Isabel and Mercedes were sitting side-by-side at the coffee table in the family room, coloring in a new coloring book when Officer Phyllis Beatty arrived. A neat, middle-aged woman with improbably black hair and a cigarette smoker's wrinkles, she dropped her small overnight case in the foyer and shook Isabel's hand.

The policewoman surveyed her with sympathy. "Rough couple of days, huh?"

"Yes, ma'am." Truthfully, anxiety was eating Isabel alive. She glanced into the foyer mirror. Big mistake. She looked like the refugee she was. "The most frustrating thing is, I can't go looking for my little boy myself. I have to depend on other people to do it for me."

"We've got experienced detectives. They'll do everything they can to find him."

"Officer Beatty, I have every confidence in the Del Rio PD, but some things are just out of control."

"Please call me Phyllis," said the other woman. "I have a feeling we're going to get to know one another pretty well in the next day or two." She warmed Isabel with a surprisingly charming smile.

"Okay, Phyllis it is. I'm Isabel."

"Oh, I knew that. Agent Carmichael made it very clear you're a special case."

Isabel blushed. "He probably meant *head* case."

Phyllis laughed and walked toward the family room, unbuttoning her jacket. "And this must be Mercedes."

"Yes." Isabel beckoned Mercedes, who laid down her pink crayon and shyly came to take Isabel's hand. *Officer Beatty,* she spelled for the little girl. Mercedes gave the woman a scared look and ducked behind Isabel. "She doesn't hear or speak."

"That's what Agent Carmichael said. Too bad, but deaf kids can be really smart in other ways."

"She is," Isabel said. "And a very talented artist." *Show your pictures?* she signed for Mercedes.

Looking relieved to be dismissed, Mercedes scooted for the stairs.

Isabel gestured for the policewoman to sit down. Soft leather furniture and large plants, a skylight, and a wide-screen TV made Pamela's den a comfortable and inviting room. As prisons went, it was an okay place to be.

Phyllis made herself at home, tossing her jacket across the arm of a rocker. "Agent Carmichael suspects this may be a kidnapping. Your boy—Danilo's his name, right?—he's been missing for over twelve hours?"

"That's right." Nauseating fear assailed Isabel again.

"Does your hostess suspect Mercedes was the one they were going for?"

"No. At least I hope not." Isabel wasn't sure any longer just who knew what. She was pretty sure she could depend on Pamela's discretion, but Eli had insisted on keeping her out of the loop.

"Where is Mrs. Hatcher right now?"

"She's heading up a charity organization meeting at a local women's shelter. She knew you were coming, but she thinks your presence is just a precaution." Isabel put shaking fingers to her temples, partly to shield her expression from the officer. "I hate lying—"

"That's because you're a good person," said Phyllis. "Most people don't have a bit of problem with it."

Agitated, Isabel grabbed the TV remote and flicked it on. Oprah began to hold forth on the latest fad diet. Isabel might be a basically good person, but she wasn't nearly smart enough to deal with this situation. How could she have let Danilo out of her sight? It was her fault he was gone.

Chapter Eleven

Mercedes stood at the foot of the stairs, clutching her sketch pad. She knew enough English to understand the lady officer's words all too well. Danilo had been kidnapped, and it was *her* fault he had been taken.

I'm the one they wanted.

Fear clenched her stomach. Pablo had found her again. First he'd killed Lupe, then burned down Isabel's house. Now he'd stolen away the little brother God had given her.

If she could only undo that silly game last night. Danilo didn't know how to get away from Pablo.

She was going to have to show him.

Just then Isabel looked around and smiled. *Come here.*

Mercedes obeyed, climbing onto the sofa between the two women. She let Isabel take the sketch pad and flip through it with Officer Beatty. She had more important things to think about than pictures right now, so she jumped when Isabel squeezed her knee, just hard enough to get her attention.

Isabel was pointing to a portrait Mercedes had drawn last night. *Who is this?*

Mercedes shrugged.

Eli parked in front of the ruins of Isabel's house and sat there looking at it. With the house and all her memories burned up, nothing held her in Del Rio anymore. Once she got the insurance paperwork straightened out, she had no reason to stay.

Immediately he felt ashamed of the thought. He should want the best for Isabel. If she wanted to leave and go back to college, who was he to wish less for her? Isabel deserved the best, but she'd lost everything important to her. Her husband, her house and now even her little boy.

Eli got out of the vehicle and walked up to the scorched mess that had been Isabel's home. As a crime scene, it had been roped off, picked over and investigated both by the fire department and local police. It had been determined that the fire started with a bowl of gasoline placed near the pilot light for the hot-water heater. The fire alarm was in perfect working order, but the battery had been disconnected.

The thought of some criminal entering Isabel's house sickened Eli.

Eli crouched on the blackened sidewalk in front of the porch. He could close his eyes and see Fonzie snoozing beside the steps. Too bad about the dog. One more thing Isabel had lost.

"Hello? Officer!"

Jolted out of his thoughts, Eli looked over his shoulder. Isabel's elderly neighbor, Mrs. Peterson, stood on her porch across the street, waving at him. She was actually the person he'd come out here to talk to, on a tip from police who had interviewed the neighbors after the fire. He'd met the lady only once, but Isabel spoke highly of her and her husband's kindness.

He rose and crossed the street. "Hi, Mrs. Peterson."

She stuck on a pair of glasses that had been hanging from a chain around her neck. "Oh, Eli, it's you!" She moved down the porch steps one slow step at a time. "I've been trying to call someone from the city about our garbage pickup."

Amused that he had been relegated from federal agent to "someone from the city," Eli grinned and met the old lady at the end of the sidewalk. "Sorry, I don't do garbage, but I needed to talk to you about something else."

Mrs. Peterson stopped and put a bony hand to her chest. "Whew! Looks like I need to get back on my treadmill. What can I do for you?"

"Listen, Mrs. Peterson, I know you talked to the police after the fire. But would you go through it again for me? I'm trying to piece together everything we've got."

"I just remember you and your brother taking Isabel and the children off for the day. I thought to myself, well, good for Isabel, she deserves a day out, and I came in to watch my soaps and mind my own business." Mrs. Peterson frowned a little. "'Course, first I had to make that meter-reader fellow move his van so the mailman could get to my mailbox."

On the point of walking away, Eli stilled. "Was he anybody you'd ever seen before? What did he look like?"

"Hispanic. Heavyset, I guess, and wearing sunglasses. Had on one of those blue jumpsuits." She pushed up her glasses. "I'd never seen him before."

"So you talked to him? Do you think you could describe him to a police artist?"

"I don't know. Maybe. But you know my vision's not what it used to be."

Since the old lady's eyes behind the lenses of her glasses were magnified to the size of golf balls, Eli could well believe it. "Look, Mrs. Peterson, would you go with me down to the station and look at some pictures, see if you recognize the guy?"

"Well, sure." Mrs. Peterson looked pleased that somebody thought she had something important to say. "Howard doesn't like people blocking our mailbox."

"Where is Mr. Peterson, by the way? I'd like to talk to him, too."

"He's on the golf course. Can't hit a lick at a snake, but he thinks he's Tiger Woods. Just let me go spackle on a little paint and I'll go with you." She turned to toddle back toward the house.

Feeling more hopeful than he had in days, Eli went back to the car to wait. He'd been praying for a break, and if Mrs. Peterson could ID the arsonist, this just might be it.

Isabel sat down at the breakfast bar and studied the pencil portrait Mercedes had shown her. Its simplicity and economy of line gave it had an almost pen-and-ink quality. But though the girl in the drawing's beautiful face was very young, she was posed chin down, looking up with a sultry expression that was anything but childlike. Dressed in a ruffled off-the-shoulder blouse, with gaudy jewelry and extravagant makeup, she looked like nothing so much as a teenage prostitute.

Isabel grieved all over again for Mercedes, who obviously knew this young woman well. What kind of life had she lived before running away to the orphanage?

While Mrs. Peterson was looking at a computer file of smugglers, Eli went back to his office to think. Leaning back in his chair, he looked at the items lined up on his desk.

One small, blue flowered tennis shoe with bloodstains inside the heel, and one beaded bracelet.

A pearl-handled switchblade. More rusty stains.

And the last item, a child's full-color drawing of a murder scene.

Frowning, he picked it up. The psychologist who had interviewed Mercedes claimed the child showed all the typical signs of trauma. During the interview her expression remained serene, almost vacant, as though she understood not a word translated by the deaf interpreter.

He'd had a profiler look at the drawing, as well as a police artist—professionals who agreed that the child who drew it had seen something terrifying. But neither had had a point of reference to interpret place and time, or identify victim and perpetrator.

The problem was, the crime had occurred in a border slum. Life there, for vast multitudes of people, was little more than a matter of survival—and for many, a cheap quantity to be taken at will.

Eli's job was defined as an American law officer. His assignment was not alleviating the poverty and violence south of the border, but protecting the citizens of his own country. Still, he would have given anything for the power to do both. His enemy had been on U.S. soil at least twice, vulnerable to prosecution by American law, and Eli had failed to capture him.

Now, unless Mrs. Peterson's description revealed some previously unexplored clue, Eli would be forced to wait until his enemy struck again. Galling.

On a personal level, all he wanted was to love and care for one little girl, one little boy, and most especially one woman. There were no guarantees there, either; if anything, the prospect of a relationship with Isabel looked pretty hopeless at the moment.

He rubbed his forehead just above the bandage. It itched like crazy, and he had a lingering headache. He needed to talk to somebody. Needed another brain to help him analyze the evidence.

The only person he wanted to talk to right now was Isabel.

Earlier in the day Isabel would have given anything to see Eli. Now she almost wished Phyllis, self-appointed butler that she was, would slam the door in his face. How could Isabel possibly look him in the eye without telling him about the kidnapper's call?

But Officer Beatty, who seemed to have a soft spot for blue eyes, took her hand off her gun and stepped back. "Carmichael! I thought you said you'd be tied up all day."

"I need to see Isabel." A presence of barely contained energy, Eli came in and shut the door behind him. He was in uniform, as clean and pressed as ever, though a shadow of dark late-afternoon beard outlined his mouth and jaw.

Isabel wanted to fling herself into his arms.

That, or hide behind the sofa.

Phyllis gave Eli a speculative look. "Well, she's pretty busy wearing out the carpet, but I guess we could spare you a minute or two. Haven't heard a word from search-and-rescue. Do you know what's going on?"

He shook his head, his gaze finding Isabel's. "I've come about something else."

Isabel swallowed. "What is it?"

Eli hesitated, glancing at Phyllis.

"I'll give you some privacy." Phyllis plopped down in a leather recliner and turned up the volume of the TV. "But behave yourself, Carmichael," she added with a glimmer of a smile.

Eli reddened and pulled Isabel into the empty dining room. "Where's everybody else?"

"Rand hasn't gotten back yet. Pam is letting Mercedes help her cook dinner."

He nodded. "Good. Come here." He drew two chairs close and sat down in one. If Isabel sat in the other, she would be knee-to-knee with him.

Anxiety over what Danilo could be going through trumped any lingering shyness. Isabel sat down, clenching her hands. The Lord had known how much she wanted to see Eli. Now she couldn't talk to him. *Oh, God, what do I do?*

"What's the matter?" she asked.

He showed her a Ziploc bag he'd had tucked under his arm. "You haven't seen this, because I didn't think it was any big deal at the time. But—" He opened the bag and removed a cheap beaded bracelet and a small blue-flowered tennis shoe. "Mercedes was wearing these when we found her in the orphanage." Eli touched the bloodstains on the shoe. "Remember the gash on her knee?"

Isabel nodded. Mercedes had been through so much. "Where's the other shoe?"

"I don't know. I'm hoping you can help me brainstorm a little." Eli opened his wallet and pulled out a sheet of tablet paper Isabel recognized from Danilo's school supplies. "Remember this?" He unfolded the paper and showed her Mercedes's drawing.

Isabel shuddered. "How could I forget?"

"Well, I got to wondering if Mercedes has drawn or painted anything else that might give us a lead." He laid the drawing on the table, with the two items from the bag on top. "Maybe the bracelet or the shoe will jog your memory."

Isabel instantly thought of the portrait Mercedes had shown Phyllis. "She has been drawing a little since we've been here. But I don't think—" Her eyes fell on the little bracelet. Suddenly she realized that the size and shape of the beads echoed the odd, rounded foreground element in the picture. "Eli! Look at that."

"What?" He followed her gaze. "I've looked at that thing a hundred times." He jerked the drawing off the table, and the bracelet fell to the hardwood floor. Its rotten string broke, sending beads rolling everywhere.

Isabel bent and caught a handful of them, laying them against the bottom of the drawing. "Look what she's drawn here. It's not drops of water, Eli, it's beads. There are strings of them in people's doorways all over the colonies."

Eli rattled the paper, making the beads jump. "You're right. I don't know why I didn't see it."

"Beads are kind of a girl thing." She smiled a little at his chagrin. "But—I might know who the woman in the picture is. I'll show you." Isabel hurried to the den, where she'd left the portrait on the coffee table.

Phyllis looked around in concern. "Everything all right?"

"Um, yes, fine," Isabel said, distracted. She snatched up the picture and went back to the dining room. "Here." She thrust the portrait into Eli's hands.

He studied it for a long minute, then looked up at Isabel with blazing blue eyes. "When did you find this?"

"This morning when Phyllis first got here. Mercedes volunteered it, I don't know why she picked now—"

"It doesn't matter." Eli laid aside both drawings and got up to take Isabel's wrists, though he'd had her complete attention since he entered the house. His hands, big and warm and reassuring, sent electric shocks up her arm. "I remember seeing beads like that—same size, same color—in a bar I went to the other night. I'll either go back myself, or send Artemio."

"You think that's where the murder happened?" Frozen, she didn't move even when Eli unconsciously clenched his hands so hard her wrists ached.

He nodded. "There was a big storage room in the back, where I talked to Caslas, the guy who owns the place. Beads across the doorway and the room was laid out just like in her drawing. If Mercedes was there, then Caslas would have to know her and this young woman."

"Who is this girl, Eli? Mercedes won't say who she is. Maybe, if we could find her, she can lead us to Danilo."

Eli released her enough to take her by the shoulders. "I know this is my fault, Isabel. I can't tell you how sorry I am that I got you and Danilo mixed up in this. If I could go back and do things different—"

"No." Isabel looked up at him with eyes blinded by tears. Even in her grief, she couldn't let him take all the blame. "I was *meant* to care for Mercedes. She feels as much my child as Danilo."

Eli suddenly let her go, and Isabel looked around to find Phyllis Beatty standing in the doorway. "Everybody all right in here?" asked the policewoman.

"We're okay." Eli stepped back and put his hands in his pockets. He looked at Isabel as if trying to gauge her emotions. "I need to talk to Mercedes before I go. One other thing came to light today. Your neighbor across the street—"

"Mrs. Peterson?" Isabel supplied.

"Yes. She ID'd a Mexican thug who sometimes works as a bodyguard for the governor of Coahuila. From her description of his vehicle, he may have been the same guy that ran me off the road yesterday."

"How did she—"

"She saw him pretending to read meters on your street the day of the fire. He's got to be our arsonist."

"Eli, that's wonderful!" Isabel exclaimed. "You can find him, right?"

"Well, he's not smart enough to be working alone. And he's probably back across the border by now. Anyway—" Eli reached up to rub his forehead "—I want to show his picture to Mercedes, see if she recognizes him. And talk to her about this new drawing of hers."

"I'll get her, she's in the kitchen. But Eli," she said over her shoulder, "you really need to slow down. You took a bad knock on the head yesterday."

He shook his head, dropping onto the sofa. "I'll rest later."

Isabel found Mercedes standing on a chair beside Pam, who was stirring something in a pot on the stove. Pam looked around and smiled. "I heard Eli's voice. Any word?"

Isabel shook her head, not up to explaining. "He wants to talk to Mercedes."

Mercedes had already climbed down from the chair and run to hug Isabel. Isabel found it amazing that the child could be so affectionate. She must have had a loving influence somewhere in her short life.

Laying both hands on Mercedes's hair, she kissed the

child's forehead. "Eli's here," she said clearly, and pointed into the den.

Face alight, Mercedes ran for the doorway.

Pamela bumped the spoon handle against the side of the pot, then laid it in a spoon rest. "That child's going to die of grief if you and Eli don't hook up and give her a home."

She didn't want to discuss it. "We'll figure it out."

"Isabel, a blind person could see he's in love with you."

Isabel shivered involuntarily. "I can't stay in Del Rio."

"I'm just saying—"

"I've got to go back in there. Thanks for cooking dinner." Isabel hurriedly headed for the family room, forcing her friend's earth-shattering words from her brain. *He'll get over it. He just thinks he's in love because I'm the only single female he's been around lately.*

But when she walked back into the den and saw Mercedes tucked under Eli's arm, Isabel's throat closed at the tenderness of his expression. If ever Isabel had seen a natural father, here he was, right in front of her eyes. She sat down on an ottoman where she could watch the conversation between man and child.

Looking like a bright-eyed little robin in a red T-shirt and shorts, Mercedes leaned trustingly against Eli's chest. Isabel knew she enjoyed feeling the rumble of a voice against her ear.

Eli looked down into the little face tilted upward like a flower to the sun and spoke carefully in Spanish so that she could read his lips. "You know Danilo's in trouble, don't you?"

Mercedes nodded. Her lips trembled.

"I think you can help us find him," Eli said.

Mercedes scrunched her face and looked at Isabel, who translated Eli's words as best she could into sign language. Mercedes's eyes widened. *How?*

Eli looked at Isabel, then reached for the murder scene drawing that lay on the coffee table. "Remember this?"

Mercedes's lively expression shut down. She tucked her chin.

Eli tipped it back up with a gentle finger. "Mercedes, who is this?" He tapped the red-smeared, prone figure in the picture.

She shook her head and shrugged.

"Will somebody hurt you if you tell?" When she wouldn't look at his mouth, Eli said, "Isabel, ask her."

Heart pounding, Isabel moved into Mercedes's line of sight and translated Eli's question.

The little girl began to shiver, and shook her head.

Isabel knew that had to be a lie, but if Mercedes was that frightened, neither she nor Eli had any power to elicit the truth. She was afraid Eli was in a mood to somehow force a confession. There was a dangerous flaring of his fine nostrils, and he briefly closed his eyes.

"Mercedes, I won't let anybody hurt you," he said. Then he wrapped his arms completely around her and rocked her as if he were her daddy. Mercedes clung to Eli, her arms around his neck and her cheek pressed to his.

Isabel found herself caught in the oddest mixture of desolation and awareness of God's unending Father-love. *There's something here, Jesus,* she thought. *You can't take away the pain if I don't give it to You, but You hold me anyway, pain and all.*

Slowly, Mercedes loosened her hold on Eli and reached for the young girl's portrait. Picking up a stray crayon, she began to write on the bottom line of the page.

Lupe. Looking up at Isabel, she repeated the signs she'd used the night they'd been reading *How the Grinch Stole Christmas.*

My sister is dead.

Chapter Twelve

"I told you she's one tough little munchkin," Eli said, watching Mercedes walk into the kitchen holding Phyllis Beatty's hand, in search of a cookie. The revelation about her sister Lupe had seemed rather to be a relief than anything else.

Beside him, Isabel sat elbows on knees, chin cupped in her hands, studying the pair of drawings on the coffee table. She sighed. "I don't know how she survived all this, much less came out so sweet and trusting."

"Well, you know a lot of her healing is because she's had you to love her."

Isabel looked up at him and bit her lip. "Anybody would—"

"No, anybody would not." He reached over to take one of her hands. "You are a woman of God, and I—"

"Eli!" She sat up, eyes widening. "This is not the time for—"

"Maybe not," he said, "but I'm tired of waiting for the right time. Tell me why you stopped wearing your wedding ring." He ran his thumb along the fourth finger of the dainty hand cupped in his.

She jumped to her feet, snatching both hands behind her back. "That's personal."

"It sure is." He got up and stood uneasily, feeling like the biggest heel on the planet, but determined not to be a coward any longer. "It's personal to me. I want to know if there's any chance you feel the same way about me that I feel about you."

For a split second he saw something luminous and hungry flash in her eyes before she looked down. "Don't push me, Eli. I can't take it right now."

There was fear in her voice, real enough that he wanted to take back his question and assure her he hadn't meant anything by it. He couldn't do that, but he knew he'd run head-on into some emotional wall.

He looked at her for a minute, longing to hold her. He didn't know if it was wisdom or his own fear holding him back. "Okay," he finally said, and took a breath. "Okay. I won't ask again until you come to me." Isabel swallowed. When she didn't answer, he picked up Mercedes's two drawings. "I'm going over to Acuña to show these to Artemio. Call me if you hear anything on Nilo."

"All right," Isabel said quietly.

Decided that was all he was going to get out of her, Eli headed for the door. Sometimes, apparently, God just plain said *no*.

* * *

Isabel walked through the kitchen, headed for the deck outside.

Pamela, standing inside the refrigerator door, looked around. "Are you all about ready for supper?"

Isabel looked at her blankly and kept going. "I'm sorry, I'm not hungry."

"Isabel?"

But Isabel shut the door behind her and stood looking blindly at the pool cleaner chugging like a rubber snake across the water.

She couldn't talk to Pamela about this thing with Eli. She couldn't even articulate it to herself. How could he question her about her...feelings, when her little boy was being held hostage by a known murderer? If she'd put her rings back on, or if she'd just explained to him that she hadn't wanted people to think they were married—she could have cut it off right then and there.

Instead, she'd avoided the question, let him think there might be hope that she'd—

That she'd what? Fallen in love with him?

"I can't go through that again," she muttered, pushing her hands into her hair, leaning over to ease the ache in her stomach. Losing Rico had been bad enough. Getting used to being without him, learning to deal on her own. "God, if I have to love somebody, why can't You give me some nice, safe tax accountant or something?"

Unexpectedly, the idea made her laugh. She clapped her hand over her mouth to stifle a rather hysterical giggle.

And then a giddy bubble of elation floated up from her toes all the way to her scalp.

Eli loves me.

He'd been about to say it before she stopped him. Pamela was right, it was in his eyes and the way he touched her and his tender care for her.

I won't ask again, he'd said.

And she could not offer herself to him. She could not.

"That's Lupe Serraño," said Artemio, flipping the drawing back across the table. "Little hooker we kept trying to get off the streets until she disappeared a couple of weeks ago."

Eli picked up the paper and once more studied the clean pencil lines Mercedes had sketched. Her sister. Knowing the life of a Mexican prostitute, he would have said the two were more likely mother and daughter. The girl looked to be about eighteen, but she was probably in her early twenties.

Not that it really mattered. If Lupe was dead, Mercedes was an orphan in every sense of the word.

"What do you know about her?" asked Eli.

He had met Artemio in one of their usual spots, an all-night grocery-cum-liquor store on the outer edge of downtown Acuña. Temio was dressed in his typical nondescript black and brown, his dark hair covered by a black bandana. For himself, Eli figured at this point a uniform would be nonproductive, so he'd gone to his locker at the station and quickly donned an old pair of jeans and a brown T-shirt.

Artemio flicked a finger at the back of the picture.

"Always standing on a street corner waiting for a man. She seemed to favor Anglos coming over for a good time. You can see she was really pretty, so she could afford to be a little picky."

"You didn't know she had a little sister?"

"These girls—their families usually throw them out the first time they get pregnant. Then they're on the street, no place to go, so they just start living the life." Temio's expression darkened. "So, no, I'd have no way of knowing anything about their families."

"Okay. But we've got her and Bryan Hatcher, both murdered—probably in Caslas's joint. Then we've got Isabel's house burned down and her boy missing. We've got to assume Mercedes is the connection."

"Yeah." Artemio rubbed his chin. "Anything turn up with the arson investigation?"

"Point of origin was the laundry room. A bowl of gasoline near the water-heater pilot, and it ignited in the middle of the night. A neighbor ID'd a guy entering the yard as a meter reader."

Artemio sat up. "There ya go. Who was it?"

"Thug named Camino. He was in Mexico City with the governor of Coahuila the night of the murder. We're looking for him."

"You don't think the governor's in on this, do you?"

"I hope not." Eli rubbed his aching head with both hands. "Point is, we've got a dead hooker, a dead oil baron's son, and now a little boy missing, probably kidnapped. And Temio—" he looked up "—this kid feels like my own son. We've got to connect the dots fast."

Artemio smiled a little. "Well, you've saved my skin more than once. I'll do what I can to help."

"All right, then find me a hooker who knew Lupe Serraño."

Isabel quietly shut the bathroom door before she turned on the light. She didn't want to wake Mercedes.

Leaning back against the door, she reached into the pocket of the short terry robe Pamela had loaned her yesterday. No, the day before. She closed her eyes. The last week had blurred into one long nightmare. She had no idea what day of the week it was. Was it even June anymore?

Looking at the digital clock on the cell phone Eli had given her, she saw that it was almost midnight, and her stomach gave a little lurch. She turned on the shower to muffle the sound of her voice. If she woke anybody up, they'd think Isabel was a little weird, taking a shower in the middle of the night, but at least she'd be left alone. Then she closed the lid of the toilet and sat down to wait.

Twice she started to dial Eli's number only to immediately cancel it. All her life she'd relied on the authority of law enforcement, especially as the wife of a federal agent. Only the memory of the dreadful phrase *I will kill your son* kept her from following her instincts. She couldn't take the chance.

Suddenly the phone's display panel lit. Shaking so badly she could hardly hold on to it, she flipped it open. "Hello?"

"Are you ready to trade?" asked the distorted voice.

"Where?"

"Cross the border and go through Acuña. At the south highway, head west into the mountains. After twenty miles, you will see an abandoned cement factory. I will call in three hours. Bring the little girl, nobody else. Do you understand me?"

Isabel could hardly force her lips to move. "I understand."

"Remember, if you bring the police he dies."

Closing the phone and clenching it in her hand, Isabel bowed her head. *Oh, Jesus. My enemy surrounds me.* Tears dripped on her bare knees and ran down her legs. *Please protect my baby and give me strength to get to him.*

She shuddered. *Father, what do I do about Mercedes? I can't surrender her to this murderer.*

Even if she managed to get out of the house without waking Officer Beatty—who slept in a guest room down the hall—how was she going to get her car? It had been hidden, locked in the Hatchers' barn.

"God, this is too big for me," she whispered. She sat up, pulling free a length of toilet paper in order to wipe her face and blow her nose. After a moment, sudden anger steadied her. "I *will* figure this out," she muttered.

Then she looked at the phone. Its message light blinked.

She snatched the phone open, and this time there was a face on the screen. A little round face with messy black hair and scared brown eyes, above a red T-shirt.

Isabel froze, clutching the phone.

* * *

Eli left his car parked in a lighted lot behind one of the restaurants in downtown Acuña that catered to Americans. From there he let Artemio drive his ancient Dodge Dart to St. Teresa, mostly to save wear and tear on his Jeep. Besides, Temio knew the rabbit warren of streets like he knew his own tattoos, and drove like a stunt man. Time was short.

Artemio stopped the car at the bottom of the hill with a final roar of the unmuffled engine. He grinned when Eli made an exaggerated check of his teeth to make sure none had jarred loose. "You Americans got no sense of adventure."

"Facing a grizzly at ten paces is adventure. Riding with you is kamikaze." Eli wrestled the door open and got out of the car. He looked up at *Las Joyas Bellas* and shook his head. At just past midnight, the place was literally rocking. Music boomed from every window and the open door, and Eli could hear scuffling and glass breaking in counterpoint. "I didn't see any girls last time I was here," he said, following Temio up the hill.

"You probably came too late," said Temio. "Much later than this, and they're all hooked up." He suddenly turned and caught Eli's arm. *"Español, amigo,"* he said quietly, "and let me take the lead." He continued to the open doorway.

Ten minutes later Eli was sitting at a table, working hard at keeping his eyes above the neck of a young Mexican girl dressed in…well, not much, if his first glance at her was anything to go by. She was very pretty, in a sloppy kind of way, and looked him boldly in the eye. She kept scooting her chair toward him, then he'd move away, until he was nearly sitting on top of a laughing Artemio.

Finally Artemio had pity on Eli, slapping a ten-peso bill onto the table and holding it until he got the girl's attention. "Sylvia," he said, "my friend is very shy, so you will leave him alone. All we want to do tonight is talk."

Sylvia pouted. "Talk is boring, and your friend is cute."

Artemio rolled his eyes. "I promise you my conversation is interesting enough to keep you out of jail, if you tell me what I want to know. Eh?"

Her thick black brows drew together. "I don't know why I'd have to go to jail. I haven't done anything."

"We'll see." Artemio scrubbed the money back and forth a couple of times. "Did you know a girl named Lupe Serraño who used to work here?"

Sylvia twirled her hair. "I knew Lupe, but I haven't seen her in a while."

"Do you know what happened to her little sister?"

"Mercedes? No, she disappeared about the same time as Lupe." Sylvia shrugged. "Maybe they went with her boyfriend after all. Lupe sure talked about him enough. He said he was some kind of big-stuff bodyguard."

"Bodyguard?" Eli, easily following the conversation, couldn't keep his mouth shut. "You mean Camino?"

Sylvia giggled. "That fat pig? No, he was only Pablo's flunky."

Eli started, and Artemio gave him a warning look. "Where can we find Pablo? Does he work for the governor, too?"

"Why?" Sylvia looked suddenly alarmed. "You won't tell him I mentioned his name, will you? Bad temper, that one."

"I've forgotten all about you, *querida*," Artemio assured her. "Have you seen…what was his name?"

Sylvia hesitated until Eli slid another bill across the table. "Pablo Medieros," she mumbled. "I've got to get out of here. I don't feel good." She hitched her purse onto her shoulder and darted toward the door.

Eli leaned toward Temio. "Can you run the name for me? I want to know everything about this guy."

"Sure. But I'll have to do it myself. Not sure who I can trust." Artemio looked uncharacteristically worried. "If this guy's on the governor's staff—"

"I know. Look, find out what you can and come back for me. I'm going to talk to Caslas again, look around the area."

Artemio nodded. "Watch yourself, though. This place is a snake pit."

As his compadre pushed through the crowd, Eli approached the bar. Different bartender tonight; not surprising, this place had a short life cycle.

"Where can I find Hector Caslas?" Eli showed the bartender another bill, much smaller than the one he'd given the hooker.

The money disappeared. "That's an easy one. Caslas is dead."

Dumbfounded, Eli looked around the noisy, smoky room. "But—"

The bartender shrugged. "Life goes on."

"What happened to Caslas?"

"Got on somebody's bad side, I guess." The bartender slung a filthy rag across his shoulder and leaned in for gossip. "He was watching TV with his wife last night, somebody calls his name, and he goes to the door. *Bam!*" The bartender slapped his chest, shaking his head. "Shot, standing right there in his house."

"Man." Eli stepped back. Another possible witness eliminated. Medieros, if he was their man, apparently headed up a vicious and powerful syndicate. No wonder Sylvia had been nervous.

Fear for Danilo momentarily paralyzed Eli. This type of investigation was a whole different ball game than what he was used to. Every time he got hold of one end of the string, three more appeared to confuse him. How was he supposed to proceed now?

Consumed by his thoughts, Eli faded through the crowded tables until he found himself at the back of the barroom. He realized he stood directly in front of the beaded curtain that led to the storeroom. Mercedes's beaded curtain.

He looked over his shoulder. Nobody was paying any attention to him. With slow, inconspicuous movements, he pushed aside the strands closest to the doorjamb and slipped through.

The light of the single naked bulb in the low ceiling revealed that the room was unoccupied. Realizing he'd been holding his breath, Eli took a moment to orient himself. There'd been something in this room that had snagged his instincts last time—something more than the curtain itself. The layout of the room—it was just as Mercedes had drawn it.

He pictured Mercedes sitting in this dismal little room, trying to draw or read while her sister turned tricks in the bar. Looking through the curtain, he saw exactly what she must have seen: garish red light and movement behind the shimmering beads—almost an underwater scene.

He checked the furniture to see if anything had been moved since the last time he was here. The table and chairs were right where they'd been, as were the cot and the bench against the wall. Okay, so he was going to move things himself, look under everything.

First the table. After shoving it aside, he got down on his knees to examine the tile floor. It was stained, imperfectly laid, but yielded no clues. Frustrated, he walked over to the cot. Quickly he stripped the bedding, then flipped the whole thing over to look underneath. His heart jerked when he found a couple of books—children's books in English, with the covers ripped off and pages dog-eared. Evidence that perhaps Mercedes had been here, but nothing to do with the murder.

The only thing left was the bench, simply constructed from a two-by-four plank and a couple of cinderblocks. He lifted the plank, and what he saw made him fling himself to his knees. Near the floor, underneath where the bench had been, the tar-paper wall had been ripped open to form a flap, sort of like a doggie door. Eli cautiously pushed against it, putting himself inside the skin of a scared little girl. He could easily imagine Mercedes shimmying through this flap as a matter of convenience, or a way of escape. As his hand dropped, it brushed against a bent nail, wickedly placed at the juncture of floor and wall—maybe the source of the gash in Mercedes's knee. It was amazing that she hadn't developed tetanus as a result.

Okay. Now what?

Eli searched the shadows close to the wall, unsure of what exactly he was looking for. He moved one of the cinderblocks and sucked in a breath. Behind it was a small blue-flowered tennis shoe, a perfect match to the one Mercedes had been wearing when he found her. If she had been here and witnessed the scene in her drawing, it would explain why Medieros was determined to get rid of her.

Eli stuck the shoe in his back pocket and made sure everything in the room was back where he'd found it. He slipped back into the barroom without attracting attention, taking a deep breath when he hit the relatively fresh air outside.

He pulled out his cell phone to call Artemio and nearly had a heart attack when it suddenly vibrated in his hand.

"Eli, you're not going to believe this," said Artemio. "Hector Caslas is dead."

Mercedes sat up in bed. She'd been awake long before she felt Isabel get up. She had a decision to make, and she knew God was talking to her.

She didn't like to think about the night her sister died, because Lupe had been so frightened and her death so violent. And remembering her heel in Pablo's hand…a nightmare. But now she understood why she'd had to tell Eli about it. If she'd told a long time ago, Danilo wouldn't have been taken from his mama.

The anxiety in Eli's blue eyes had made Mercedes want to cry. The trouble was, even after she'd told him about Lupe, it didn't seem to make him any happier. If anything he'd looked even more grim.

She knew Pablo wanted her, Mercedes, instead of Danilo. No telling how many other people Pablo would hurt to get to her.

She slid out of bed and crept toward the bathroom door. She put her hand to it and felt the warmth from the shower steam seeping through the cracks. Isabel was getting ready to do something brave and dangerous, she could feel it.

God, please let me help her. Here I am.

She got up and found her sandals, then sat down on the floor to put them on.

Chapter Thirteen

Eli knew it was late, but he called his supervisory agent's home number anyway. Now that he had Pablo Medieros's name, he wasn't going to let anything keep him from finding the guy.

"Carmichael, have you completely lost it?" snarled Dean when Eli identified himself. "It's one o'clock in the morning!"

"Yes, sir. But I think I've found the Mexican mobster who's the source of all that coke funneling through our sector. He killed Bryan Hatcher and—I suspect he kidnapped the Valenzuela boy. Owen and I want to take the hilo across the river to get him."

"I'm dealing with lunatics. No wonder Washington keeps turning down funding. You know perfectly well you can't cross the border in a government helicopter, they'll shoot you down and put you in prison." Dean paused. "And rightfully so."

"The *federalies* have *asked* me in." Eli made an effort

to monitor his words. "Respectfully, sir, you assigned me to stop the leak, and I've found a way to do it."

Eli was suddenly aware that Dean was fully awake, fully engaged, and mad as a nest full of hornets. "Are you questioning my judgment?"

"Sir, I—I know you told me to stay out of the Hatcher murder, but it's connected to my other case. If there's a good reason why Owen and I can't go across to look for the Valenzuela boy, you need to tell me what it is."

Dean hesitated. "I'm taking care of it myself."

Eli pressed. "Let me at least tell you what I've found out. Did you know that the governor of Coahuila's personal bodyguard is trafficking—"

"That's the point," Dean ground out. "There are political ramifications you can't begin to understand. Trade negotiations between us and Mexico are delicate, and right now both our jobs depend on making Washington happy."

"But, sir—"

"Carmichael, do what you have to do. We never had this conversation."

Eli watched the disconnect light blink. Then he realized Dean had said in so many words that he could go.

Rico had always said that if the family livelihood depended on Isabel's acting ability, they'd be on food stamps within a week. It was a good thing she didn't have to deal with this in daylight.

Turning off the shower, then the light, she stumbled through the dark room toward the bed. She knelt beside it, trembling so hard the mattress shook. Mercedes was going to wake up thinking an earthquake had erupted.

She remembered telling Eli that she was a home-maker not a warrior—or some such drivel. Well, she was certainly proving that out.

Call Eli. She slipped her hand into her pocket and closed her fist around the cell phone. But what if she did that, and the kidnapper found out she'd disobeyed orders? Still, she flipped open the phone and located Eli's cell number. She could trust him to tell her the right thing to do.

Before she could rethink it any more, she pushed the call button. Two rings and she heard an electronic message, "The cellular number you have dialed is currently unavailable for service."

Okay, so the decision was out of her hands, at least for a while.

Clenching the bedspread, she stayed on her knees for a while longer, agonizing over what she knew she had to do.

She was going to have to leave Mercedes here and go across the border, hoping she'd know what to do once she got there. Isabel reached for Mercedes.

All she touched was a cool, empty bedsheet.

She stopped herself on the point of screaming. Biting her lip hard, she found the bedside lamp and turned the switch.

There was Mercedes, sitting cross-legged in front of the door. She was dressed in the red shorts and shirt and her new sandals.

Weak-kneed with relief, Isabel collapsed onto the bed. "Mercedes, what are you doing? You're supposed to be asleep." She mimed sleeping with her hands against her cheek.

Mercedes got up. *I'll go with you,* she signed.

"No, baby. Come here." Mercedes reluctantly approached, and stood knee-to-knee with Isabel. "I have to go look for Danilo. You stay."

The big brown eyes watered as Mercedes shook her head.

"Yes." Isabel tried to look stern, though her heart was breaking. "I promise I'll come back. Obey Officer Beatty and Pamela."

Dark. Night, Mercedes signed.

"Yes. Go back to sleep." Isabel grabbed Mercedes in a hug, then picked her up to lay her in the bed. *I love you,* she signed, then reached for the lamp switch.

Isabel walked through the quiet, softly lit house into the kitchen, where she found a pen and paper. She wrote a brief note for Pamela, asking her to care for Mercedes until she returned and promising she'd be back in a day or two. She left it propped against the coffeepot.

She started a second note addressed to Eli, then thought better of it. He'd likely come looking for her anyway, and she didn't know if that was a good thing or a bad thing. She wadded the note and threw it in the trash can under the sink. She couldn't leave a note and take the chance that somebody she didn't trust might find it.

She hooked her purse strap over her shoulder and dug

out her keys. Breathing a prayer, she left the house by the kitchen door.

Mercedes slid down off the bed and followed Isabel down the stairs, staying far enough behind so as not to get caught. When Isabel went into the kitchen, Mercedes scooted through the den into the foyer, then out the front door.

She had seen Isabel's car in the barn the night Danilo disappeared. In fact, she'd almost decided to hide there, but found herself lured by the kittens instead.

Now she knew exactly how to get there.

She trotted through the moonlit pasture between the Hatcher's landscaped yard and the outbuildings, pausing only to climb over a fence post. *Good thing I'm fast,* she thought.

Fast but not obedient, an ugly little voice in her head whispered. *Worse than Danilo. Isabel will spank you when she finds you out of bed.*

Mercedes ran faster.

She reached the barn and paused to look over her shoulder. Isabel still wasn't in sight, and Mercedes panicked at the thought of being out here alone all night long. What if Isabel decided not to come for her car?

Well, she thought, *you've been in worse places before.*

Determined not to be left behind, she gritted her teeth and walked around the corner of the building until she found the small opening she'd seen the cats going in and out of. Wriggling and squeezing, she managed to get through it.

Ugh—the barn was dark, doubly frightening because of the horses. She wouldn't see it if one of them came at her suddenly. With her insides quaking, she sidled along, her eyes gradually adjusting to the darkness until she made out the dim outline of the car at the far end of the center aisle.

Relief poured through her as she ran the final steps to the vehicle. At least the car was safe and familiar. Yanking open the rear door, she hopped in, slammed it shut and squeezed into the floorboard space between the front and back seats. Fortunately, the overhead light was broken, so Isabel wouldn't see her back here until it was too late.

It would be worth a spanking to be with Isabel.

As Isabel hurried across the pasture, silence pressed down on her shoulders like an anvil. If she strained, she could see the lights of the international bridge ten miles away. It had been a long time since she'd been out alone this late at night. Fear pierced the numbness she'd wrapped around herself since Danilo was taken.

God, please take care of him and Mercedes. Help me know what to do.

With everything in her she wished Eli were here to share this burden, this fear. How had she gotten to be so emotionally dependent on one man's strength? How could a slow baritone voice be so reassuring, and at the same time make her heart race? Sometimes, with Rico, she'd felt as much like a parent as a wife. Eli made her feel completely like a woman. Better and stronger and more aware of God's presence in her life.

Isabel began to walk faster, as if to outrun the dangerous longings that had overtaken her common sense.

A few minutes later she stood in front of the Hatchers' barn, staring at the padlock in the hasp across its door. She had her car keys, but how was she going to get into the barn?

Think, Isabel. If you were a brave, resourceful woman, what would you do?

She walked around the building looking for a way in. It was constructed in typical fashion of rough unpainted boards, and well-ventilated, but the windows were near the tin roof. Even if she'd had a ladder, Isabel knew she'd break her neck climbing down from the inside.

That obviously wasn't going to work.

But when she rounded the corner of the barn, the gleam of an ax propped against a woodpile caught her gaze. *Thank You, Lord.* She grabbed it, staggering a bit as she ran back to the front of the building. Either it was heavier than she'd expected, or she was extraordinarily tired. Maybe both.

She stood looking at the lock, nervously swinging the ax in both hands. She'd never had a reason to pick one up before, and she could just imagine the noise this procedure was going to make. She looked around to make sure she was alone.

Oh, yeah. Nobody here but us chickens.

Gritting her teeth, she drew the ax back in perfect batting stance as she'd seen Eli demonstrating for Danilo. Feet apart, knees bent, elbows up.

Here we go. She swung with all her strength.

To her astonishment and joy, the blade bit into the lock dead center, split the hasp in two, and stuck in the door.

"Wow," she muttered. "Grand slam."

With one quick yank she had the door open, and there was her little Escort sitting in the center aisle of the barn. It was darker than the Seminole Canyon caves in here, but she knew this vehicle like the back of her hand. Fishing her keys out of her pocket, she ran to open the driver's door.

Making arrangements for Owen to fly the chopper across the border turned out to be a bit more complicated than Eli had bargained for. Artemio was highly connected in the police force, but the number of officials he could trust were limited. Eli found himself cooling his heels in a cantina for nearly an hour, waiting for permission to land the helicopter without bringing the wrath of the *federales* down on his head.

To keep from going to sleep, he decided to fill the time by harassing Phyllis Beatty.

"Phyllis, this is Eli," he said when she groggily answered the phone. "Sorry to call so late, but I need a favor."

"What's the matter," she teased, "you border boys run out of yards to roll?"

He chuckled. "Listen, do me a favor and go down the hall to check on Isabel, would you?"

"Do it yourself, Don Juan."

"Phyllis…" He dragged her name out teasingly. "Please? I'm tied up for the foreseeable future, and I'm worried about her. But don't wake her up if she's asleep."

"Oh, all right," she grumbled. "But you owe me a steak dinner. Hold on."

Eli could hear her footsteps on the hardwood floor, heard her yawn and open a door. Then a distinct gasp came over the line. "Eli, she's not in the bed. Neither is Mercedes. Let me check the bathroom." A few seconds later, Phyllis's voice returned, slightly strained. "I can't find her. Listen, I'm going to check downstairs. She probably couldn't sleep and went down to watch TV or something. Let me call you back."

Before Eli could reply, the connection ended. He closed his phone and stared at the neon Pepsi sign on the opposite wall. Somehow he'd known something was wrong.

The lump of lead in his stomach wasn't going away anytime soon.

Isabel reached the customs checkpoint on the bridge and offered her driver's license to the agent. She recognized the young Hispanic man with neat mustache and dimples as a co-worker of Rico's who'd been in their home a time or two.

"Isabel!" he exclaimed. "What're you doing out this time of night?"

If she told Berto that her son was being held by a kidnapper, he'd probably call the men in white coats. She tried not to look suspicious. "My grandmother's ill, and I've been called to help care for her."

Telling lies was getting altogether too easy. Maybe she should be worried about her morals.

"Where does she live?" asked Berto.

"Ten miles or so out in the country, on the other side of Acuña."

"Okay." He flicked his flashlight beam across her lap to the passenger seat. "When do you plan to return?"

"I— It's kind of an emergency. I'm not sure."

Berto handed back her driver's license and turned off the flashlight. "You should be careful. There are a lot of drunks and crazies running around this time of night." When Isabel started to roll the window back up, he put out a hand. "Wait, would you like an escort?"

Isabel's heart hammered. "No. No, thank you. I'll be fine, I've driven it a million times."

He gave her a searching look. "Hope your grandma gets better soon."

"Thank you." Isabel rolled the window up.

Oh Lord, please forgive me.

Tied hand and foot, Danilo Valenzuela lay blessedly asleep on a pallet in the corner. His superhero nonsense, amusing at first, had driven Pablo right over the edge. On the verge of cutting the boy's tongue out, he had finally taped his mouth again.

He turned as Camino entered the camp's great-room, throwing the screen door back on its hinges and then slamming it shut again with a great bang.

"*Hola,* Pablo," sang out Camino, yanking a chair away from the table. He straddled it backward and propped his arms across the top. "You wanted to know when the woman crossed the border." He reached in his shirt pocket for a pack of cigarettes. "She is on her way."

Pablo didn't know whether to smack his *compadre* across the back of the head or embrace him. "And the *niña?*"

Camino looked offended. "Our man on the bridge saw her in the back seat. Can you not trust me?"

Pablo approached the table and laid his palms flat in order to make his well-developed muscles bulge against his shirt. "You were going to be sure she died in the house fire, and look how *that* turned out. If you'd done your job right, we wouldn't be in this fix right now, with my ears numb from listening to this kid ask questions!"

Camino scowled. "What am I, a certified arson specialist? I'm a *bodyguard.* Here, you can fix your problems with a gun. In *el norte* it's not so simple."

Pablo ignored this ridiculous, whining excuse. "And when I tell you to take care of the Border Patrol agent what do you do? You give him a bump on the head."

"A bump that would have killed any normal man." Camino gestured wildly with a cigarette as if it were a conductor's baton. "I tell you, Pablo, these people have some sort of magic charm protecting them. I do not know what you think you can do against such luck."

"Luck, bah!" Pablo slammed his hand against the table, making Camino jump. "I make my own luck. I have one more job for you."

"I've been out all night. I'm hungry."

"You can fill your fat stomach after you find a place to put the boy while I talk to the woman."

Camino glanced at the boy. "Why? She'll be more likely to do what you want if she sees the kid."

"I, unlike you, plan for all eventualities," Pablo snarled. "I don't trust her to leave the police out of it, and I'm not taking a chance on losing my hostage if things go south."

"Oh, all right," Camino said, heaving himself out of the chair. He lumbered over to the boy, picked him up, and slung him over his shoulder. "Don't worry, I know just the place."

The Escort jolted over the bumpy streets of Ciudad Acuña as Isabel twisted and turned her way through the city. At the fork on the south side, she chose the westbound highway.

The terrain grew more and more rocky and desolate, the highway winding between dark, looming hills. The waning moon cast small, broken shadows at the feet of the occasional cottonwood tree or mesquite bush as her headlights flashed across them. Houses and barns—poor, tumbledown buildings made of cinderblocks or plywood—were few and far between. What livestock Isabel saw reminded her of the starving cows in Potiphar's dreams.

Watching the odometer, she slowed when she'd driven about nineteen miles and started looking for the cement factory mentioned by the kidnapper. There it was. She checked the clock on the radio. She was about thirty minutes early, which meant she had a long, nerve-racking wait in the dark on this deserted highway.

Father, I'm sorry for being angry with You earlier. I don't know anything. I don't know why You've let me go through this valley of fear. All I can do is hang on to You. All I can do is—

She heard a sneeze. A muffled, but distinct sneeze coming from the back seat. Heart bumping, she pulled into the gravel road leading to the factory and stopped. She knew what she was afraid of, but prayed she was wrong.

Getting up on her knees, she leaned over and reached down. Her hand came in contact with a silky mass of hair and two small hands over a face. She closed her eyes in dismay. "Mercedes, you didn't… Oh, what am I going to do now?"

Chapter Fourteen

It was nearly four a.m., with the sun beginning to turn gray over the eastern horizon, by the time the chopper lifted off with a jerk and a sway. Eli's stomach lurched. He wasn't exactly acrophobic, but he'd never enjoyed the adrenaline rush of flying the way Owen did.

By aerial view, the Rio Grande twisted through the hills, outlined by spots of weak light that resembled the markings of a rattlesnake. Closing his eyes to shut out the nausea-inducing sight of the ground receding into a black dot beneath, Eli adjusted the headphones to a more comfortable position. He could hear Owen talking to the control tower in Piedras Negras, discussing wind shear, altitude and flight pattern, but he tried to concentrate on how he was going to find Medieros.

Artemio had discovered that Medieros's boss, Governor Avila, had a military base in the hills west of Acuña, where militia groups trained at odd seasons. Nobody could prove it, but DEA had long suspected they hired out as mercenaries for the drug cartels operating on both sides of the border. Medieros was apparently pretty high on the organization's food chain.

Eli certainly had enough to occupy his thoughts. Still, he had a hard time keeping his mind off Isabel.

Phyllis had radioed through headquarters ten minutes after cutting him off, to say that Isabel had left a note in the kitchen. Unhelpful at best, it had simply said she would be back in a day or two. An equally vague note, addressed to Eli and unfinished, had been found in the trash. Phyllis didn't know what to make of the fact that Mercedes had disappeared as well.

He knew having his attention divided was dangerous, but he couldn't control the worry that gnawed at his stomach. Where could Isabel and Mercedes have disappeared to?

Hampered not only by the darkness, but by the natural camouflage of the hills, they kept having to fly lower than even Owen, cowboy that he was, found comfortable.

"I think Artemio's playing pin-the-helicopter-on-the-map-of-Mexico," Owen growled, banking left, a hair's breadth away from a flat-topped mesa that had seemingly sprung up out of nowhere. "Get him on the radio again."

Eli squinted through the binoculars. "The GPS says we're close. Make one more pass—"

Suddenly the radio crackled in the headset. "Headquarters to Broncbuster, come in."

Marlon Dean. Eli clenched his fists.

Owen lifted the chopper and set it to hover. "HQ, this is Broncbuster."

"What's your twenty?"

"We're about fifteen miles south-southwest of Acuña."

"Good. Get your brother on the mike."

"I'm here," said Eli. "What's up?"

"How much do you know about the situation at the Hatchers'?" asked Dean.

Not knowing how far Dean could be trusted, Eli hesitated. "I'm aware of a problem there," he said carefully.

"It's more than a problem." Dean paused. "It looks like your lady has taken things into her own hands."

"What do you mean, sir?" Eli looked at Owen, whose mouth hung open.

"Berto Guillermo passed her through the checkpoint on the bridge an hour or so ago. He almost didn't report it, but something she said didn't ring true, so he did some checking. Thank God he called me. I don't know where she's going, but if she's in contact with the kidnapper, things are going to get dicey."

"What do you want us to do?"

"I'm going to send you straight to Avila's camp. I want you to bring them both out alive."

"How do you know—"

"Carmichael, I admit I've given you a hard time because I didn't quite trust you, but I've been keeping an eye on this situation all along. How do you think you got permission to take that chopper across the border?"

Eli exchanged glances with Owen. "Hold on a minute, HQ," he said, and flipped the transmitter so that only Owen could hear him. "You think he's straight up?"

Owen shook his head. "Don't know. My gut wants to trust him."

Eli stared out into the slate-blue sky. The thought of Isabel driving into Medieros's camp, with or without Mercedes, made his blood turn to ice. He didn't want to believe it was possible. "Owen, Dean could be leading us into an ambush. The guy's been trying to get rid of me ever since he transferred in."

"Say the word and I'll turn the radio off. We'll keep looking."

What it boiled down to, Eli supposed, was faith. There were very few people on the planet that he'd trust his *own* life to, much less that of Isabel and Danilo.

Since he was probably going to get fired anyway, he readjusted the radio so that Dean could hear him. "Give me one reason to believe you."

Even over the radio, Eli could hear the tenseness in Dean's voice. "You know Petrarca reports directly to Avila," he said. "I've been working with them for nearly a year, trying to bring down Medieros. I know exactly where he is."

Before she got out of the car, Isabel surveyed her surroundings. She'd halfway expected the kidnapper to have somebody waiting for her here. But there was not another vehicle in sight. All she saw, looming above her like a horror movie set, were the steel-and-concrete towers of the factory. Thank God, she still had some time before the kidnapper would call.

Okay, deal with Mercedes first. Opening the back

door, she helped Mercedes out of the car. Isabel pulled the little girl close, dismayed at the rigid, defensive posture. "It's okay, I'm not mad," she mumbled, mostly to herself, stroking Mercedes's hair reassuringly. "But what am I going to do with you?"

There was no way under the sun she could bring the child with her any farther. If she did, the kidnapper would have no incentive to release Danilo.

It followed, then, that she would have to somehow hide Mercedes before he called.

Isabel's gaze was drawn again to the monstrous shape of the factory. It looked like it hadn't been in use for quite some time. One entire wing had collapsed, and huge sections of the roof were ripped away. Only the central tower seemed intact.

Is that where I should take her? Oh, God, she'll be so terrified if I leave her here. Why couldn't she have stayed with Pamela like I told her to?

With sudden clarity Isabel realized that her own self-protective behavior often got her into trouble as well. *Father, is this the kind of obedience You get from me? Please help me know Your will right now.*

She didn't get a bolt of lightning or a pillar of cloud to lead her, but somehow peace filled her as she led Mercedes by the hand toward the building. She stopped in front of the steel double-door and stood there looking at it, squeezing Mercedes's hand. What would she do if it was locked?

Just a little bit of faith, that was all she needed. She grabbed the door handle and yanked. It opened easily, and she looked over her shoulder to make sure they were really alone.

Yes. Taking a deep breath she entered the building with Mercedes. She found herself in a cavernous concrete entryway with a broken front window that revealed dust motes circling in a shaft of early-morning light. The foyer rose at least three stories, with a set of iron stairs leading to a railed mezzanine circling the second floor. It was truly a bizarre structure, but Mexican architecture was often almost free-form, compared to modern American engineering.

She looked down at Mercedes, forcing a confident smile. "Let's find a place for you to wait." When her voice bounced back at her, she looked around nervously. She didn't see or hear anybody else.

Shuddering, Isabel led Mercedes toward a door labeled *"oficina,"* opening off the entryway. She tried the door, found it unlocked, and walked into a small office sparsely furnished with a cheap desk and chair. A couple of rickety crates sat under a tiny window which admitted just enough light to make the dingy room depressing, but not scary.

Mercedes slipped her hand out of Isabel's and signed, *I wait here.*

Yes. You wait. Isabel knelt and hugged Mercedes again, then did her best to explain in sign language that she had to be a brave girl and pray for Danilo.

Mercedes's bottom lip trembled, but she looked up at Isabel with trusting brown eyes. *I'm sorry I not obey,* she signed. *I love you.*

Isabel repeated the sign back to Mercedes, trying hard to smile. *I forgive,* she signed. *I'll come back. Don't leave for any reason.*

Mercedes nodded; then, with a poise staggering in one so young, she walked around the desk to sit in the chair. *I obey.*

Choked with tears, Isabel shut the office door behind her. There was no way to lock it, so she'd have to trust God to guard Mercedes until she could come back for her.

As she left the building, a chilling question occurred to her. What if she didn't make it back? And what if the kidnapper searched the factory?

What if she and Danilo both were murdered, leaving Mercedes abandoned in this godforsaken place? Isabel swallowed against a lump of dread. *You can't have brought me this far to leave me.*

But how could she make sure Eli would be able to find Mercedes if, God forbid, Isabel didn't make it out alive?

She could try calling him again.

The kidnapper had said no law enforcement interference, but there was no way Eli could get here before she went in. Her hand was being forced, though she couldn't say whether it was by God or the adversary.

Call him.

She hadn't been able to reach him earlier, and she was in an even more remote area now.

Try, Isabel.

Only fifteen minutes remained before the kidnapper was to call. Shaking in her haste, she pulled the phone out of her pocket and dialed Eli's cell phone number. *The cellular customer you have dialed is currently unavailable....*

In tears, she canceled the connection. Okay, now what?

Phyllis. Maybe she could find him. Eli had made her save the number before he left.

She sagged in relief when Phyllis answered immediately. "Beatty here."

"Phyllis, it's Isabel. I need to get hold of Eli, but he's not answering his cell. Do you know where he is?"

"Are you all right? Where are you?" Phyllis demanded.

"I'm...perfectly fine," Isabel said. "I just had an errand, an emergency. Please help me find—"

"He's looking for you, hold on and I'll patch you through."

To her astonishment and joy, a minute later she heard Eli's voice.

"Isabel, where are you?" His voice was rough with anxiety.

"I'm in Mexico. Mercedes is with me—I have to put her someplace safe. I want you to know where, in case—"

"Yes, but wait for me, I'm coming to get—" His voice was interrupted by static, and Isabel panicked.

"I can't wait, he'll kill Danilo."

Apparently he heard her just fine. "Isabel, don't you dare go in there by yourself!" She'd never heard Eli raise his voice before. He sounded like a crazy man.

"I have to. Listen, I didn't mean to bring Mercedes, but she hid in my car. So I'm leaving her in an abandoned cement factory on the southwest highway, nineteen miles outside town. You can pick her up here when this is all over."

"Isabel—"

"I've got to go now. Eli, I—I love you."

"Wait!"

Isabel closed the phone.

Lord, please help him forgive me, she thought as she walked back to her car.

"She loves me," Eli said numbly, staring at Owen. "I'm going to kill her."

"News flash," his brother said irritably, "everybody in Texas got that message but you."

"Owen, she's going into Medieros's camp alone. Apparently she's almost there. We can't get there in time."

Owen's expression turned grim. "Then we'll just have to hurry."

Isabel's cell phone rang at the exact moment the clock on the radio changed from 4:59 to five o'clock.

She somehow managed to find a calm voice to answer. "Hello?"

Now that he had her on this side of the border, the kidnapper had apparently decided voice distortion was no longer necessary.

"Mrs. Valenzuela. I am looking forward to meeting you," he said in Spanish-accented but clear English. His friendly tone made Isabel want to hurl the phone out the window. She took a hissing breath through her teeth, and he chuckled. "I am going to give you instructions on how to get here. You are at the concrete factory, correct?"

"Yes." She couldn't make herself be polite, indeed saw no reason to.

"Ah, perfect. You are a most resourceful young woman. I congratulate you. I trust you have taken good care of my little friend Mercedes. I can't wait to see her again."

Isabel closed her eyes, breathing hard. "I want to speak to Danilo."

"I'm deeply sorry, but that is not possible right now. You will be able to speak to him soon enough. Wait in your car. My men will arrive shortly."

Fifteen minutes later a battered green pickup drove out of the mountains. Already frozen with terror, Isabel hardly registered the barrel of a rifle pointing at her from the passenger window. The truck rattled to a stop beside her car, and the driver—a wiry Mexican dressed in brown camouflage—got out. His taller companion kept the gun trained at her head.

"Good morning, *señora*," said the driver in English. "I am Ortiz, and I will be your escort today." He laughed as if he had made a fine joke. "Delgado, if you will please tie the *señora's* hands I will— Wait." He looked around, frowning. "Where is the *niña?*"

"I left her in the trunk as I was told to."

He seemed not surprised that Isabel would be the kind of person who would tie up a seven-year-old child and leave her in the suffocating heat of a car trunk. "All right, just leave her there. I will drive your car. We do not want anyone to steal it, heh?" He grinned at her. "Delgado, look in the trunk to make sure the good *señora* is telling us the truth."

Isabel nearly vomited. She had prayed he would be too lazy to look. She got out of the car, ready to try to grab the gun or some equally foolish stunt, but Ortiz grabbed her hands as the taller man wrenched her keys from the ignition and popped the trunk.

Isabel stifled a whimper as she saw the bag of balls and bats Eli had left in her trunk last week. With Isabel's plaid picnic blanket tossed over it, the bag looked exactly like the outline of a child. But if he moved it…

"She's here," said Delgado, slamming the trunk.

Isabel's knees buckled in relief, and Ortiz yanked her upright, tugging her around to the passenger side. He pulled a bandanna out of his pocket and proceeded to tie it tightly across her eyes, blindfolding her. He then tied her hands with stout rope. "Come on, get in." He shoved her into the car. "We're late. Delgado, you lead in the truck, and I'll follow."

Isabel felt the car turn and turn again, snaking around hairpin bends that took her farther and farther from Mercedes and closer to Danilo. Through the open windows, dust churned off the rutted dirt roads, making breathing even more difficult through the cloth over her eyes and nose. Miserable and afraid, she endured.

Ten minutes later, by her estimation, the vehicle stopped with a jerk and final gasp of the old engine. She heard the driver's door open, and a moment later her captor was yanking her out of the truck. He took off the blindfold but left the rope around her wrists, and she found herself inside a six-foot chain-link fence with electric barbed wire across the top. In the distance she could make out a dark clump of barrackslike structures. It looked like a prison camp.

Please, Lord, let Danilo be all right.

She looked around to get her bearings. The sun was coming up across the top of the mountains, flooding the landscape with a surreal, dreamlike glow. Behind her little blue car sat the ugly green truck. Delgado had already gotten out, with the rifle now carelessly flipped over his shoulder.

"Get the girl out of the trunk," Ortiz ordered, popping the trunk with the remote button on the key chain.

Isabel braced herself, but Delgado's roar of rage still had her cowering back against her car. Spanish curses echoed in the predawn stillness as he tossed the blanket and mesh bag of baseball equipment onto the ground.

Ortiz dragged Isabel with him as he stormed around to the rear of her car. "What are you doing, you moron?" he demanded in furious Spanish. "Where's the—" He whirled to glare at Isabel in patent outrage. "There is no child here!"

She lifted her chin. "That's right. I left her back in Acuña. I came to get my son, and I won't give up Mercedes until he's safely out of here."

Ortiz hit her across the face, splitting her lip. Isabel gasped in pain.

"Pablo said we weren't to hurt her," cautioned Delgado. "She's worth a lot of money."

"Pardon me if I don't care what Pablo said," snarled Ortiz. "She made a fool out of us."

Without another word the men marched her toward the barracks, their booted feet kicking up choking puffs of dust. By now Isabel was so tired her legs quivered, and she only kept herself erect by praying for Danilo, Mercedes and herself.

Some twenty yards past the compound, she saw a two-story building, very different from the one-room barracks. A deep porch crossed the front of the structure, which resembled a hunting cabin where she'd once vacationed with Rico. Distracted, she stumbled on a crooked paving stone, fell to her knees and tore her jeans on a sharp rock. She cried out, painfully jerking her arm out of her captor's grasp. She knelt there, breathing hard, utterly out of her depth.

Her prayers were incoherent.

Ortiz hauled her to her feet again and pulled her up onto the porch of the two-story building. Banging on the door with the butt of his gun, he waited until someone answered, then shoved Isabel inside. She staggered, but managed to stay on her feet.

"Ah, Mrs. Valenzuela, you have finally arrived. Welcome." The voice was smooth and familiar: it was the one she'd heard over the phone.

A young Hispanic man, sleek black hair gelled and brushed away from a high forehead, rose from behind a massive desk. Sloe-black eyes and a fitly muscled

body brought him into the realm of model material. His
cunning expression made her skin crawl.

She took an instinctive step backward. "Where's
my son?"

"He has been asking for you." The man's eyes trav-
eled down her figure and back up to linger on her face.
"I'd forgotten what a pretty lady you are." A slight smile
curved his mouth.

Isabel shuddered in revulsion. "Who are you?"

"Someone who knows how to get what I want." He
slid his hands into the pockets of immaculate dark
gray trousers. In spite of the summer heat, his black
silk shirt was buttoned all the way to the throat.
"Come, let's do business." He looked over her shoulder, at his underling. "Ortiz, where did you put the little girl?"

"She tricked us," mumbled Ortiz, sending Isabel a
venomous look. "She says she left the kid in Acuña."

The leader's expression darkened with rage. "Is
this true?"

"I'll tell you where she is when I know my son is
safe." Isabel couldn't keep her voice from shaking.
"Where is he?"

The man clicked his tongue. "Your little superhero
has been right here, sleeping and watching television.
However, a little while ago we moved him, just in case
you decided to get foolish." He walked over to grab Isabel's arm. "Which it appears you have."

She tried to yank free, merely succeeding in collect-
ing a bone-deep bruise.

"See what you have brought on yourself?" The leader clicked his tongue, gesturing toward the doorway.

Turning, Isabel saw the shadowy outlines of a silent army in dun-colored camouflage uniforms—men with large, heavy guns. She had not thought beyond this moment; now she realized she was in no way prepared to outthink or outmaneuver this evil force.

Chapter Fifteen

"This is very poor planning, yard boy," said Owen as he set the chopper down gently on a shallow hillock tucked between two larger bulges of the Acuña mountains. They'd had to be careful about a landing spot. Close enough to save travel time, but not so close that the helicopter's approach would alert the enemy. "We're way too close to the road."

"Tell me something I don't know." Eli was in the middle of checking his gun. "I wish we had time to look in on Mercedes. Make sure she's really in a safe place."

Owen cut the engine, leaving sudden, stark silence. "Isabel wouldn't leave her exposed."

"Not on purpose, for sure. But what if Medieros has men on patrol?"

Owen removed his headset and hooked it in place against the instrument panel. He tugged a brown knit cap over his blond hair. "You know she did what she had to do. Dude, talk about a rock and a hard place."

"Which is why we've got to hurry. Come on, let's go." Eli climbed into the back of the chopper and started gathering supplies and ammo.

A few minutes later Eli and Owen were jogging side by side down a steep hill toward the highway. Carrying backpacks filled with ammunition, they both wore equipment belts, onto which were strapped the usual accoutrements: pistol and knife, radio and cell phone, compass, field glasses and a small tool kit. With Artemio's express permission, both men carried AK-47s on the left shoulder.

According to the GPS, they were about a mile from Medieros's camp, and making good time. Eli glanced at his brother. Owen's usually sunny expression had grown gradually more grim as they neared their destination.

Halfway up another grueling hill, Owen caught Eli's glance. "Somebody's been working out," he said with a smirk. "Trying to impress a lady?"

"Some women are more impressed by brains than a six-pack."

Owen laughed. "Some of us have both."

They ran in silence for a few minutes. In other circumstances, Eli would have enjoyed the exercise and fresh air. This undeveloped part of Mexico had its charm. Sunflowers bloomed in patches, nearly hidden by cactus and mesquite, and the occasional cottonwood twisted in the elegant lines of modern sculpture. Eli watched an eagle circle overhead, looking for breakfast.

The obvious Bible verse from Isaiah 40 came to mind. He'd learned it a long time ago, and never forgot it. *"They that wait upon the Lord shall renew their strength. They shall mount up with wings as eagles. They shall run and not be weary, and shall walk and not faint."*

He could use a little of that strength.

"Hey, Eli, you ever think about what made Dad turn his back on everything?"

Eli glanced at his brother in surprise. Owen rarely volunteered introspection. "Sometimes," he admitted. "Why?"

"Isabel asked me one time if we'd had any warning that he was going to do what he did." Owen uttered a harsh laugh. "I kind of blew her off, but I keep thinking about it. You know…what makes one man a hero and another man a goat."

"I guess everybody's got potential to heave off to the dark side. That's why we need Christ."

"I just wanted you to know I'm not as goofy and shallow as I seem. In case something happens to us out here, and I don't get another chance to tell you…" Owen paused, and Eli waited, curious. "I want you to know I love you, and I admire you more than anybody I know."

Eli couldn't speak for a moment. "Thanks, that means a lot. I love you, too." He cleared his throat. "And for the record, I don't think you're shallow. You just need the right girl to give you a little direction."

Owen snorted. "That'll be the day. Are you and Isabel gonna hook up? When all this is over, I mean?"

Eli wasn't much for baring his soul, particularly to his little brother, and he'd already said a lot. But the circumstances seemed to call for honesty. "I love her more than life. But for some reason, she doesn't want another Border cop for a husband."

"Have you asked her?"

Ignoring him, Eli lifted his field glasses. "I think we're getting close."

"I know," said Owen. "'Shut up, Owen. None of your business, Owen.'"

Eli just grinned. "There's a reason I was born first."

Medieros pushed the woman into a camp chair, then sat down behind the governor's magnificent mahogany desk. He steepled his fingers under his chin.

"You have hurt yourself," he observed, noticing a cut on her knee exposed by the rip in her jeans. It wasn't bleeding a lot, but dirt and gravel had penetrated the skin.

"Your concern overwhelms me," she muttered without looking at him.

He noticed again that she had a nice shape; it was too bad she was such a modest dresser. "A small scrape of the knee is the least of your problems, I think."

Isabel Valenzuela just gave him a stony stare.

Pablo looked at his slim gold watch. "We are running out of time," he said, switching to Spanish as he spoke to Ortiz. "Are you sure the little girl is not in the car?"

Ortiz scratched his oily head. "We searched it. She didn't bring the kid."

"She hid her somewhere else. Go back and look." Pablo wished he could afford a brighter subordinate.

Ortiz looked confused. "There's that cement factory about a few miles outside camp. But it doesn't look like a place this lady would leave a little child."

Pablo eyed the woman coldly and said in English, "Where is the girl? Did you leave her in the factory?"

She answered in perfect Spanish. "I said I would tell you as soon as I know my son is safe." She raised her chin, looking absurdly small and defiant.

Which gave Pablo a certain thrill. What pleasure to make her bow to him. He got up from his chair, enjoying the slight widening of those beautiful dark eyes as he walked around the desk. "Ortiz, send Delgado to search the factory. And shut the door."

Mercedes didn't like this place.

It was nearly as gloomy as the storeroom of Hector's bar, and it smelled musty. A snake or a tarantula might be living in one of those rotten crates. She knew how to get rid of scorpions—in her old life with Lupe, she had often found them climbing in her bedclothes—but she couldn't stand spiders. Mercedes would do just about anything Isabel asked her, but if a tarantula came to visit she was outta here.

She knew why she'd been left. She could tell from Isabel's worried brown eyes that she didn't like it, either. But Isabel had said she would come back. Mercedes knew it was a promise.

Having had a nice long nap in the back of the car, she wasn't sleepy. It was a good thing, because the coils of this old chair sprang out of the split upholstery, giving her unexpected digs every time she moved. Still, it was better than sitting on the dirty floor.

She didn't have a doll to play with, or paper to draw on, so she entertained herself by making up a story.

The silent princess spent her days alone in the highest tower of a faraway castle. Nobody heard the beautiful music she made by strumming the strands of her midnight hair. One day, she thought, the prince will hear me. He will climb the ivy and sing the song and say "My bride! I love you—"

Mercedes stiffened. Something black, about the size of one of Danilo's baseballs, had scuttled out from behind the largest crate and darted into the shadowy corner nearby. The hair on the back of her neck rose.

I can't stay here with that thing. It's big. Help me, Dios!

She pulled her knees up to her chest and watched the corner for movement.

Why couldn't Isabel have taken her along? She would have stayed out of the way. Maybe she could run and catch up. But first she had to find a way out of this building without stepping on that spider or one of his family. The door seemed like a long way off, and the crate blocked her route to the window.

Keeping an eye on the spider's corner, she edged toward the door. *Dios, help me!*

Halfway there she saw the tarantula move. Without looking to see where he went, she ran for the door and yanked it open, then pelted through the atrium and out into the sunshine.

* * *

Following Dean's directions, Eli and Owen shunned the road and followed a little stream that gave water to a few trees and sporadic cacti. It led upward onto the mountain where, supposedly, Medieros had holed up.

The stream was gradually turning into a deep gulch, and Eli prayed they wouldn't have to cross it. His lungs burned from the long run. He glanced at Owen, who ran a step ahead of him, his easy lope not slacking one iota on the steep grade.

Lord, please don't tell me I'm getting too old for this.

"How much farther?" Owen tossed over his shoulder.

"Should be just over that—" Eli grabbed his brother's arm as a fence line appeared at the horizon. "There. Stop. I want to radio Artemio, find out where he is."

"Good idea." Owen pulled the canteen off his belt and took a slug of water.

Eli unclipped the radio. "Ironhorse to *el Pájaro Rojo*, come in."

After a moment it crackled, and Artemio's voice said, "This is *el Pájaro Rojo*. Where are you?"

"Just outside Medieros's compound. Any idea what kind of arsenal we're dealing with?"

"He's holding automatic assault rifles and submachine guns. Don't go in until we get there."

"How far away are you?"

"Twenty miles or so. The terrain's bad, so it's taking us longer than we figured."

"We'll just check it out. I'll radio again when I'm in the clear."

"Good. *El Pájaro Rojo,* over and out."

Eli hooked the radio back on his belt and looked at Owen.

Owen grinned. "We're going in, aren't we?"

The sunflower patch wasn't very big, but neither was Mercedes. She crouched inside it, the scratchy leaves making her legs itch like crazy as she watched the big, ugly *hombre* tramping down the road toward the factory.

She couldn't have explained the overwhelming urge to hide that had sent her running away from the road like a jackrabbit a few minutes ago. But she was glad she'd obeyed her impulse. The man carried a rifle, with lots of bullets strapped around his waist and over his shoulder.

Shivering, Mercedes counted to a hundred twice, then peeked between the sunflower stalks. The man had disappeared beyond the next hill. *Gracias, Jesus.*

She cautiously stood, scratching her knees, looked both ways, then continued in the direction the man had come from. She hoped Mr. Tarantula took a big bite out of him.

Alone in the office with her ankles cuffed to the legs of the chair, Isabel had plenty of time to think about the advisability—or lack thereof—of her actions.

After his henchmen left, her captor had, with slow enjoyment, searched her clothes and found nothing. Scowling, he'd proceeded to shackle her to the chair. "Please let me know if I can do anything to make your stay more comfortable," he'd said with exquisite irony. Then he'd left the room.

She should have waited for Eli, no matter what the kidnapper said.

Father, I'll never run past You again. I need You to show me a way out of this. I need You to protect Danilo and send—

The thought jerked to a halt. Did she want God to send Eli to rescue her? Specifically him, or just *somebody?*

Suddenly she knew with perfect clarity that she wanted the blue eyes and bashful smile and big, strong shoulders of Eli Carmichael. But if she was ever going to have the chance to tell him how much he meant to her, she was going to have to be smart and careful and open to the Holy Spirit's guidance.

Composing herself, she took a deep breath. "*Señor,*" she called, "I'm ready to talk."

Eli and Owen accomplished the last quarter mile of their approach to Medieros's camp snake fashion, belly-to-ground, in about thirty minutes. Mental pictures of Isabel in the hands of a psychopathic killer had Eli sweating like a racehorse, in spite of the lack of humidity. He had to force himself not to scramble to his feet and storm the place. Slow, steady and silent, that was the way to go.

With Eli now in the lead, they finally topped a small rise, and he saw weak sunlight glinting on metal. A fence. Eli's pulse thundered in his ears. *Please, Lord, lead us.*

A quick look around revealed that they were at the back side of the compound, right where Dean had suggested would be the safest place to enter. Cupped by hills, the camp sat in the center of a shallow bowl, and as expected most of the buildings were bunched in clumps of tin roofs and cinderblock walls with curtainless windows. A two-story cabin stood off by itself, with a small storage shed behind. To Eli's relief, whatever guards Medieros retained were apparently occupied at the front of the camp.

He crawled forward and cautiously examined the fence. "Electric," he whispered to Owen. "Can you neutralize it?"

"Sure." Owen, the more electronically gifted of the two, poked through his tool kit. "Help me up on your shoulders."

Eli crouched to hoist his brother, then stood impatiently while Owen worked on the fence.

"I knew the cheerleader thing in college would come in handy," Owen murmured as he jumped to the ground.

"Wearing a chicken costume is not cheerleading."

"It was a bald eagle, not a chicken."

"Whatever. So I'm not gonna be electrocuted if I cut through the fence?"

"No." Owen paused. "Unless I got red and green mixed up."

"You get me killed and I'm gonna tell Mom." By this time they were inside the fence. He grabbed Owen's elbow to keep him from charging toward the closest building. "Let's split up. We don't know if Danilo and Isabel are together. You go left, I'll go right. If you find one of them signal, and I'll do the same."

"Right."

"And Owen. Pray hard. If at all possible, we need Artemio to get here before the thing goes down. Don't do anything dumb, okay?"

Owen snorted. "You are such a big brother." He dropped to his belly and crawled off.

Eli decided to go for speed rather than caution. Stooped over, he ran down the slope, heading for a skinny tree about halfway to the closest building. He made it safely and peered around the tree. Only thirty yards or so to go.

After another dash he wound up at the back of the building, then crept along the concrete wall until he came to a window covered with tar paper. The sound of a silky male voice carried clearly through the window. "I am so happy you have decided to make things easier for yourself and your son. Naturally one little Mexican brat can mean nothing to you, compared to your own flesh and blood."

Isabel's voice made Eli straighten abruptly. "I didn't say I wanted to make you happy, *Señor*. I just said we were going to talk."

Mercedes knew that Isabel would not leave her with a tarantula on purpose. She could not have stayed one minute more in that room where there might be a whole nest of them. In fact, by now she had run a pretty good distance to get away from it.

Then there'd been that scary man, who almost looked like a spider himself, with his big black mustache and stringy black hair. She looked over her shoulder to make sure he wasn't following her.

What had he been doing, walking down the road with such a big gun? He'd been headed toward the building with the spiders. Had he somehow found out she was there? Good thing she'd left.

Guiltily, she thought of Isabel, who had told her in no uncertain terms to stay where she was. *I said I wouldn't disobey again, Jesus.*

Mercedes slowed her steps. Maybe she should go back.

No, I'm not going back to that spider!

Isabel always told Danilo, *Children obey your parents in the Lord, for this is right.*

Isabel wasn't her mother, not really.

But Mercedes wished she was. If she obeyed, maybe God would give her a mother like Isabel.

What about the man with the gun?

Isabel said if you did what the Lord said, He would take care of you.

Tears leaked out of her eyelids. *But I don't want to, God.*

She stopped walking.

Chapter Sixteen

Taser gun drawn, Eli moved silently along the side of the building. Medieros would have at least two guards posted outside, maybe more. If he was going to do this alone, he knew he had to make as little noise as possible while taking them out. *God, please, please help.*

At the corner of the building, he paused, leading with the gun, and stepped out. Sure enough, a guard sat with his back to Eli on the porch rail—a single guard, smoking a cigarette, his rifle negligently pointed at the ground. Eli simply walked up behind him, pushed the gun against his back and zapped him. The man jerked and fell noiselessly backward onto the dirt. Eli quickly tied and gagged him.

One down.

He waited, kneeling in the shadow under the porch rail. *Patience.* He couldn't get in a big hurry and risk alerting Medieros. A minute went by. Three, then five. Surely there was another guard. Medieros wouldn't be stupid enough to gamble on such flimsy defense.

Suddenly the door opened, and he could hear raised voices again. He got a glimpse of Isabel, seated in a chair in the middle of the room. It looked like an office, and its florescent light emphasized the pallor of her cheeks. She must be terrified.

Then a dark, smoothly handsome young man—presumably Medieros—stuck his head outside. "Ortiz!" he yelled. "Has Delgado come back yet?" He waited a second, and when there was no answer, repeated, "Ortiz!"

Eli could only assume that the unfortunate Ortiz was the man he had just rendered unconscious, at present lying peacefully under the porch.

"Your army seems to have deserted you," observed Isabel.

"Ortiz is an idiot," snarled Medieros over his shoulder, "but I have plenty of others to replace him." But Eli noticed the insecure pucker between Medieros's thick brows.

Eli wondered who the missing Delgado was, and where he'd gone. He tensed, expecting another guard to round the building at any moment. Medieros remained in the open doorway. Eli could have easily taken him out with his pistol, but there was Isabel right behind him.

He would have to wait. Maybe Owen would reappear soon.

Isabel watched the leader's shoulders tighten as he stood in the doorway looking like a cobra poised to strike. He was not as confident as he would like to appear, which made him infinitely more dangerous.

If Delgado came back without Mercedes, this man

would kill her. Or even worse, take out his anger on Danilo. Equally unbearable was the thought that he might have found Mercedes in the factory.

"Señor," she said loudly, "Delgado won't find Mercedes, but I have a compromise to offer. I will tell you where she is hidden if you will first take me to Danilo. I want to see with my own eyes that he's okay."

He whirled to face her. "I have a better solution. I will just kill you right now, and then the boy."

Isabel had never confronted such unadulterated evil in a human being. She briefly closed her eyes to steady herself. "Then you'll be right back where you started. Besides," she shrugged, "I have nothing to lose. My husband is dead. If you kill me I go to be with him in heaven."

The man spat on the floor. "That for heaven." He folded his arms and leaned on the door frame, a mocking smile curling his mouth. "You lie anyway. I've seen you with *la migra,* the big clown who thinks it is romantic to look at childish drawings on the walls of a cave."

Isabel felt every square inch of her body flush in outrage. "You followed us to Seminole Canyon?"

"I am a very thorough man, *señora.* Which is why you and I are going to take a little walk down the road. You have ten minutes to show me where you have hidden the *niña,* before I blow your son's head off. *Comprende?"*

Mercedes was very sorry, but the tarantula won.

She had continued trotting uphill along the road, keeping a nervous eye out for more creepy crawlies, until over the rise she saw the top of a wire fence. Now she had a decision to make.

She dropped to her stomach in the weeds beside the road. She was hot, itchy and thirsty, but she wanted Isabel with a yearning above anything she'd ever experienced.

Isabel was inside that fence, she knew it with desperate certainty.

And so was Pablo. She'd never told Isabel or Eli his name because of her bone-deep terror, and look what had happened. The only way she could make up for it was to find Isabel and help her get Danilo away from Pablo.

Creeping forward on her stomach until the fence appeared again, she slowly raised her upper body. Her heart bumped when she saw Isabel's car parked a little way inside the gate. Mercedes knew she couldn't go walking in the front way.

I'm a big girl. I'll have to find another way in. Crawling to the right along the fenceline, she eventually reached the back of the camp. Pulling herself along on her elbows, she slid downhill toward the fence and saw that someone else had already entered here. The wire had been sliced upward from the bottom as if by giant scissors, then cleverly rearranged and camouflaged with weeds in order to hide the cut.

She spent a moment wondering who had done this, then decided it didn't matter. God had left her a way in, and she was going to take it. *Gracias, Jesus,* she thought as she wriggled through the opening.

She scraped the back of her arm on the ragged wire

and stopped just long enough to cry a bit, then wiped her eyes and crawled a few more yards along the inside of the fence. She was very tired, her elbows and knees cut and hurting from the rough grass and rocky ground. Maybe nobody would see her if she lay down just for a moment. She lay with her head turned toward the cabins to her left. Between the buildings she could see several men dressed like *Señor* Spider, the man who had passed her on the road earlier. They seemed to be practicing shooting, aiming their guns at a line of painted metal shapes stationed in an open field.

If the guards were busy, she could move toward the buildings without anyone seeing her. Chances were, too, the noise of the guns would cover any sound she made. Now or never. Before she had time to think about it, she got to her feet, ducked her head, and ran.

She found herself at the back of a small building, and backed against it, pausing for breath. She had no idea where Isabel would be, but she was determined to keep looking until she found her. But first she had to rest. Mercedes squatted there, absently picking rocks out of the cuts on her knees.

The wall of the little building behind her seemed to be very thin, little more than a wooden shell. It almost felt as if it quaked against her back. Imagining an army of tarantulas marching inside, setting up a rhythmic bounce, a thrill of pure terror sizzled in her stomach. Then she realized the bumping behind her was too heavy for any spider. Somebody, a *person,* was inside, banging against the wall.

She peeked around the corner of the building and almost wet her pants. An armed guard, even larger and hairier than the man from the road, stood with his back to her, fishing in his pants pocket for something. She watched as he brought out a skinny brown bottle, uncapped it, and took a long drink from it.

Mercedes ducked back behind the shed, heart pounding. She made herself sit still, though her knees screamed with pain. *Help me be quiet,* she prayed. *Get him away from here.*

She had no idea how long she waited there, frozen with fear. Finally, just when her feet had gone completely numb, she felt the bumping against her back begin again.

Curiosity suddenly outweighed fear. Mercedes risked another look around the corner and watched as her prayer was answered in front of her eyes. The big guard finished off his bottle and threw it on the ground, where it smashed into a thousand brown pieces. Then he looked to the right and left, shouldered his gun and slouched off toward the practice area. He never looked in Mercedes's direction.

When she could no longer see his retreating figure, Mercedes eased to a standing position. The rush of blood returning to her feet caused her knees to buckle with pain. She leaned against the wall, trying to catch her breath. At last, when she was able to walk, she decided it was time to see what had been shaking this building.

When she opened the flimsy door and slipped inside,

she saw Danilo crouched on the dirt floor, against the wall right where she'd been sitting. They'd been virtually back-to-back, and she'd almost been too scared to figure it out.

Mercedes dropped to her knees in front of Danilo, who looked up at her, wide-eyed with shock. His mouth, hands and feet had been secured with gray tape. She had to get him loose.

First she picked with her fingernails at the tape over his face. She almost stopped when tears seeped from his eyes and his nose began to run, but quickly realized there was no other way. With a deep breath, she yanked until the tape came off.

"Mercedes, that hurt," Danilo sobbed. She couldn't tell what else he said because he was blubbering so hard. Putting her finger to her lips to quiet him, she concentrated on his remaining bonds.

Because of the way the tape was wound around his wrists and ankles, she knew her fingers weren't strong enough to free him. She had to have something sharp. A quick survey of the shed revealed that everything useful had been removed.

Then she remembered the broken bottle right outside the door.

In a matter of moments she was sawing away at the tape on Danilo's wrists. The process was hampered when he began to wiggle and cry again. She put the chunk of glass down, shushed him with a hand across his mouth, and went back to work.

To her relief, he obeyed, shuddering at intervals as

she worked to free him without slicing him open. At last
the tape around his ankles gave.

Mercedes grabbed Danilo's hand and helped him to
his feet. His knees buckled, so she put her arm around
his waist as they left the little building.

Dios, please keep us safe.

Eli was by nature a patient man. But when Medieros's hands lingered on Isabel's ankles as he freed her,
Eli could not contain his rage.

Gun drawn, he stepped into the doorway just as Medieros grabbed Isabel under the arm and yanked her to
her feet. Isabel's gasp alerted her captor, who jabbed a
small, wicked pistol firmly in the center of her back.

"Ah, *la migra* has decided to join the party." Medieros faced Eli with Isabel clamped in front of him. "*Señora* Valenzuela, you have been a very bad girl."

"Eli, no!" she cried out.

"Medieros, I advise you not to so much as bruise her
arm." Eli steadied his own gun, training it over Isabel's
shoulder.

Medieros sighed. "I regret that I have injured the lady's
feelings, but what is a man to do when you arrogant
americanos trespass on Mexican government property?"

"No one is trespassing but you, Medieros." Eli
shifted, his gun sliding a little in a sweaty palm. Where
was Owen? "Mexican police are right outside, ready to
indict you for murder and drug trafficking. Your little
party, as you call it, is over."

"I think you do not understand who you threaten, *Se-*

ñor Carmichael." Medieros's arm tightened around Isabel. "My cousin trusts me, and there is no reason I should believe your bluff." He slid his pistol up Isabel's back until it was pointed under her ear. Eli watched her swallow and close her eyes. "Drop your gun, *señor.*"

Eli could hear Isabel's shallow breaths. He shouldn't have revealed his presence to Medieros. He should have waited for Artemio's police force, or at least Owen's signal. Medieros was like a cornered dog, and Isabel was going to get hurt.

His only hope was to keep the man talking until backup arrived. "I think it better be the other way around," Eli said as calmly as possible. "You injure an innocent American woman or a U.S. federal agent, and you're looking at life behind bars."

Medieros shook his head. "We do things different here in old Mexico, Carmichael. Family ties are very strong, and my cousin will not let anything touch me. He has his own reputation to think of." He stroked the gun barrel up and down Isabel's neck like a caress. "You wouldn't understand."

Isabel opened her eyes and looked straight at Eli. "He said he'd kill Danilo if I brought you with me." She looked like she was about to pass out. "I don't know where he is, he was going to take me—" Her voice shredded.

"Owen's looking for him," Eli assured her.

"Would you like to continue this conversation in private?" snarled Medieros sarcastically. "You will please shut up, *Señora* Valenzuela, or I will blow a hole in your pretty head."

Eli tensed, ready to spring, but a shout and a barrage of gunfire erupted outside. Eli had no idea if Artemio had arrived, or if Medieros's men had become aware of enemies on the grounds, but with Medieros momentarily distracted, Eli had a split second to react. Sign language came instinctively as he caught Isabel's gaze.

Drop.

Snatching her arm from Medieros's loosened grip, Isabel fell to her knees. She heard Eli lunging toward them, and, terrified of getting in his way, she crawled toward the desk. Gunfire still exploded outside, and confusion raged inside the office.

Isabel lunged under the desk. She could hear the two men grappling with sickening crunches of bone on flesh, thuds against the floor and walls, and furniture splintering. Her prayers rose, as frantic and incoherent as the noise around her.

Oh, God, Almighty God, I'm no heroine, but I'll do whatever You want me to do. I know You're big enough to help us.

Peace flooded Isabel, and she suddenly understood how the Psalmist had been able to write poetry while being pursued by a mortal enemy. She had trusted God for little things for her entire life. Now it was time to trust Him in something big.

She jumped when one of the men landed on top of the desk above her head. The chair behind her crashed. She turned and grabbed one of its broken legs. "Thank you, Lord, please help me," she whispered, and crawled out of her hiding place.

Isabel watched the two men fight—one tall and muscular, the other smaller and agile as a jackal. She didn't understand why they hadn't already beaten one another into a bloody mass, but they continued to stagger around the room, swinging at one another.

At last, she saw Eli step back, crouching a bit, and with a shock she realized his hands were balled into empty fists. Where was his gun? Then she saw with horror that Medieros had his own gun pointed at Eli's chest. Screaming, she swung the chair leg with all her strength at Medieros's kneecaps.

The gun went off, blasting into the ceiling as he fell backward.

Newton's third law of motion went into effect as Isabel slammed into the desk. Her head glanced off its corner, and the world went black.

Eli's every instinct urged him to grab Isabel, but Medieros was struggling onto his elbow. He had managed some time ago to snatch Eli's gun and fling it into a corner; now he lay in obvious agony, his face a mask of anger as he tried to steady his pistol.

Eli reached down and yanked it out of his hand. "It's over, Medieros. Get up."

Medieros cursed. "Your woman has made that fairly impossible," he spat. "I should have slit her throat when I had the chance."

"In that case, I'll just cuff you right where you are."

Eli took the handcuffs off his belt and knelt to lock them around Medieros's wrists. "Forgive me if I don't have a lot of sympathy for you. They'll give you an aspirin at the hospital."

"Is no problem." Medieros panted. "My men will be here momentarily I am sure, and the two of you will be back where you—"

Eli grinned when a sliding whistle chirruped from the direction of the porch. "I have a feeling my brother has eliminated that possibility as well." He turned to gather Isabel into his arms. "In here, Owen."

Chapter Seventeen

Isabel opened her eyes to find herself in Eli's arms, surrounded by half a dozen Mexican police officers. When she reached up to touch a goose egg on the back of her head, a wave of pain crashed from her ears to her tailbone. She groaned and slammed her eyelids shut again.

Which didn't help, because the lights strobing from the squad cars parked willy-nilly in the yard still somehow penetrated her brain. "Turn it off," she muttered.

"Isabel?" Eli's voice rumbled against her ear. "How're you feeling?"

"Like somebody played baseball with my head."

He chuckled. "*You're* the home run hitter, lady. Medieros may have to have knee replacements."

"You should see me swing an ax."

"What?" She heard the smile in his voice.

"Never mind. I'm so glad you're okay." She clutched his T-shirt. "Where's Danilo?"

"Getting checked out by a police medic. Mercedes found him in a tool shed and let him loose, bless her."

"*Mercedes* found him?" Isabel knew she wasn't thinking straight, but that *really* sounded wrong. "How did she get here?"

"Something about a spider. She walked all the way here by herself from the factory where you left her."

"Where's—where's Medieros?"

"On his way to jail." Eli paused and added somewhat reluctantly, "After they take him to the hospital."

Isabel sat quietly for a moment, contemplating how close she'd come to losing everything that really mattered to her. As she absorbed Eli's strength and warmth, the pain in her head began to subside.

"There's a lot I don't understand," she said, "like how you knew where I was, and how you got here so quickly. But you know, I really need to hug the children."

Eli gave her a gentle squeeze and looked at a scruffy young plain-clothes cop who, oddly, seemed to be in charge of the group of officers. "How about it, Artemio?"

The policeman glanced over his shoulder. "We've had a hard time keeping them still long enough for the medic to take a look. I'll get them."

A minute later Isabel was nearly strangled in a group hug. Danilo seemed not one whit the worse for the wear, more than compensating for Mercedes's silence with a tongue that seemed loose at both ends. "I wasn't scared a bit, Mama," he finished, sitting back on his heels to pat Isabel's cheeks. "Mercedes rescued me!"

"I'm proud of you both, honey," she said, "and I'm

so glad to have you back. But no more hide-and-seek for a long time, do you hear me?" Isabel swallowed fresh tears and somehow her stern look turned into another hug. She kissed Mercedes's cheek tenderly, thrilling when the little girl shyly returned the caress.

I love you, Mercedes signed.

"Oh, darling, I love you, too." Isabel looked up at Eli and caught an indecipherable expression in his eyes.

He looked away. "I hear Owen coming with the helicopter," he said, laying a hand on Danilo's head. "Come on, big guy, let's get your mama to the hospital. I think she needs a shot, what do you think?"

Eli had been up for so many hours straight that even the sun in his face couldn't keep him awake on the flight back to Del Rio. He woke up when the chopper's runners bumped against the Border Patrol helipad.

A team of EMTs jerked open the doors to help Isabel and Danilo into a waiting ambulance; though Mercedes was basically okay, Isabel had to be watched for signs of concussion, Danilo for post traumatic stress.

Eli himself felt like he'd been in a barroom brawl. He climbed down from the helicopter and limped over to Isabel, who was being loaded onto a stretcher. He couldn't get close enough to touch her, but stood where she could see him. "Mercedes and I'll come get you, as soon as I debrief, okay?"

"Can somebody bring me my car?" she asked. "And my phone. I need to arrange for a hotel room tonight."

Eli smiled at her annoyed expression. Isabel didn't

like to be fussed over. "We've got you covered. Relax and enjoy the ride."

"Eli—"

But the ambulance doors slammed, cutting off whatever she'd been about to say.

He stood there for a minute, feeling unaccountably desolate, but looked down when a small hand slipped into his. Mercedes smiled up at him like a ray of sunshine. He noticed one of her front teeth was coming in, giving her an oddly grown-up look. She blew him a kiss, and he winked.

Owen walked up and slung an arm around him. "You better go home and go to bed, yard boy. You look like a punch-drunk sailor."

Eli yawned. "Can't. Dean wanted to see me ASAP."

Owen's brow furrowed. "Dean needs to take a—" He glanced down at Mercedes, who was watching him with big brown eyes. "She reads lips, doesn't she? All right, I'll take her to McDonald's for breakfast and get her temporarily settled with somebody from church. Maybe take her back to Benny. Meanwhile," he whacked Eli's shoulder with mock roughness, "don't let me see your face for a full twenty-four hours."

"We'll see." Eli squeezed Mercedes's hand, and leaned down to kiss her cheek. "Be good for Uncle Owen, okay?"

She kissed him back and skipped off beside Owen in the direction of the parking lot.

"Lord, this is complicated," he muttered as he headed for the station. "Please lead me, here."

He walked into Dean's office expecting anything but the sight of silver-haired, elegantly dressed Pamela Hatcher. She sat in a metal folding chair, knees crossed and sipping coffee from a cup.

Dean pointed to an empty chair next to her. "Sit down. There are some things I can tell you, now that this is all over."

Eli sat, mostly because his legs wouldn't hold him up any longer. "Pamela?" he said stupidly. "What are you doing here?"

"I'm here to thank you for cleaning up that nest of drug dealers that destroyed my family." Eli saw her lips tremble as she hid her mouth behind the coffee cup.

"I was just doing my job." He looked at Dean, who was opening and shutting the drawer where Eli knew he stashed a box of cigars. "Did you want me to come back later?"

"No." Dean folded his arms across his lean stomach. "I brought Mrs. Hatcher in because she can fill you in on her part in this. It's fairly straightforward. She discovered her son Bryan was picking up a little spending money as one of Medieros's mules, carting drugs across the border."

Since this was no surprise to Eli, he looked at Pamela for clarification. She'd certainly kept her knowledge to herself.

She pressed her lips together. "It started when one of his friends told me he'd seen Bryan in a hot spot over in Acuña, hanging out with a prostitute and doing cocaine."

"*Las Joyas Bellas,*" Eli said.

"Yes." Pamela hung her head. "To make sure, I had Bryan followed, and that's how I found out about the drug transportation. I was devastated, because he was supposed to be in college, studying business. Rand wanted him to take over the family interests."

"That was when she came to me," said Dean. "I'll be honest, Carmichael, I didn't know you when I transferred into Del Rio Sector, and I'd heard things about your family that made me nervous. People say you have friends across the border, spend a lot of time there."

"I do missionary projects over there." Eli felt numb. Had Dean really distrusted him that much?

"Yeah, well, that kind of thing can cover up a multitude of sins." Dean rubbed his forehead. "For what it's worth, Carmichael, I owe you an apology. By the time I found out you were really the straight-up Puritan you seem to be, it was nearly too late."

Eli nodded uncertainly.

"I'm so ashamed that our son was involved in all this." Pamela looked away. "I wanted to hold him accountable for his mistakes, Rand wanted to protect him. Apparently Medieros tried to blackmail Rand, in order to find out where Mercedes was. By the time he realized the seriousness of Bryan's crimes, it was nearly too late to help. But we found some e-mails on Bryan's computer that eventually helped locate Medieros's camp." Pamela dug a tissue out of her handbag. "I contacted Agent Dean right away."

"Thank you for that." Eli knew he should feel pity for this unhappy woman, but at the moment he was too sleep-deprived to do more than lay an awkward hand on her shoulder as he rose. "Dean, may I be excused for a couple of days? And…as a favor, would you allow me to be the one to settle Mercedes Serraño's affairs? She's been through a lot for such a little girl, and I'd like to make sure she doesn't wind up back on the street."

"That's a reasonable request, Carmichael." Dean took a cigar out of the drawer and began to fidget with it. "In fact, take up to a week. We'll cover for you here. But tell your brother I need to see him no later than tomorrow morning. Something else has come up."

Too tired to be curious, Eli nodded gratefully at his dismissal and left the office. A whole week off, he thought as he limped toward the parking lot. He couldn't even remember his last vacation. Maybe he could take Isabel and the children horseback riding at his mom's place.

Come to think of it, he didn't even know if Isabel knew how to ride. He'd have to ask her.

He got in the Jeep and sat there trying to process everything he'd just learned. *Lord, You brought me through a war zone,* he thought. *Just like You said You would. Not by my own power or might, but by Your Spirit.*

So if You'd do that, I want to see what You'll do between Isabel and me.

No matter how tired he was, he couldn't go home until he knew Isabel was okay. He headed for the hospital.

Holding Danilo by the hand, Isabel came out of the ER treatment room with a whopping headache and a bunch of prescriptions. She'd been poked and prodded to the limit of her endurance. All she wanted was to go home.

Too bad she had no home to go to.

The sight of Eli, head back against the wall, snoring like a lawn mower, took the edge off her agitation. Beside him sat Owen with Mercedes in his lap, looking at the pictures in a big blue book of children's Bible stories.

When she saw Isabel, Mercedes slid off Owen's lap. Isabel knelt to grab her, heart swelling like an over-inflated balloon. How was it possible to love a child this much, a child not of her body? She'd give anything to be able to keep her.

She caught Owen's twinkling gaze. "I brought your car," he said. "You up to driving?"

"Absolutely," she said stoutly, then looked at Eli, who slept on, oblivious. "Don't wake him up until I'm gone. He needs to go home and rest before we talk."

Owen looked doubtful. "He'll murder me. Where are you going?"

"I talked to Benny. I have no money and no place to go, so we're going down to stay with her for a few days until I can get adoption proceedings started, and get my financial affairs in order. Insurance to settle and the property to sell…Benny's got room and says she could use my help."

Owen's mouth opened as if to object, then he seemed to think better of it. He grinned a little. "You do that. And let me know if there's anything I can do to help."

Isabel's gaze turned to Eli again. A longing as sharp as a physical pain stabbed through her, followed by fear, equally acute. "Tell him I'll be in touch," she said.

Eli couldn't believe Isabel had left the hospital without him. And she'd taken Mercedes, too.

He glowered at Owen, who stood over him jingling the car keys. "I'm not sure if this pain in my neck is from sleeping two hours in a plastic chair or from having to deal with you."

"Oh, really?" Owen folded his arms. "Well, let me see if I can help you figure that one out. Who's the one been flying your butt all over Mexico for the last twenty-four hours?"

Eli looked away, ashamed of his outburst. "Why'd you let her leave without waking me up?"

"Because," Owen sighed, "I could tell she's freaking out over something you're in no condition to deal with." He surveyed Eli in patent disgust. "Look at you. You look like a malaria patient."

Eli passed a hand over his face. Owen was right. Even after his nap, his eyes still felt like fine-grade sandpaper, and he was sporting a three-day beard. No telling what he smelled like.

"Okay. Point taken. I'll go home and clean up and sleep a couple hours. Where'd she go?"

"Something about helping Benny down at the orphanage until she can get adoption proceedings started."

"Sh-she wants to adopt Mercedes?"

"Apparently. I don't know why that surprises you."

Eli pushed himself to his feet and hooked an arm around his brother's neck. "Take me home, brother. I'm obviously not working on all cylinders."

Chapter Eighteen

❧

"Your turn, Mommy, your turn!" shrieked Danilo, dancing among a group of children playing in the dining hall.

Isabel, who had willingly taken on KP after supper, laughed over her shoulder as she finished wiping down a counter. She shook her head. "Benny's turn."

Benny looked up from teaching Julio DeGarmo to tie his tennis shoes. "You're the one who taught me this game. Show us how it's done."

"Oh, all right!" Isabel took off her apron and allowed the children to lead her to the open play area.

"Okay, Mom, you sit on the stool and be the puppet, and I'll be your voice. Mercedes is gonna move your arms."

Isabel's mother had taught her to play *la títere* as a preschooler, and she had always loved the traditional Mexican game. As the puppet she had the easy part. All she had to do was sit like a rag doll.

She'd been in a rather melancholy mood for the last couple of days. Helping Benny care for the children was as natural as breathing, but she knew she couldn't stay. Her mother had called every day wanting to know when she'd be driving up to San Antonio.

So far Isabel had put her off, claiming insurance settlement delays and meetings with her real estate agent. But if she planned to move to San Antonio, she needed to get the children settled in well before school started. That would be here before she knew it.

The real problem was that she didn't want to leave at all. Benny, naturally enough, had begged her to stay, and Isabel supposed she could. Food and housing would be taken care of, and Benny had even found a sponsor to support a small salary. Besides, she was hoping to adopt Mercedes. International adoptions could take up to a year, and it might be expedited if Isabel could stay in Mexico. Danilo's schooling would be a drawback, unless Isabel homeschooled him. That held its appealing aspects, but still…

Really, the whole decision-making process gave Isabel an enormous headache. Every time she sat down to list pluses and minuses of going or staying on paper, it came down to a pair of blue eyes.

If I go, I leave him behind. If I stay, I have to deal with having pushed him away.

She had told him she loved him straight-out, and he hadn't even bothered to call after he'd fallen asleep in the ER waiting room. Maybe she'd misunderstood his feelings for her. He'd never said he loved her in so many words.

"Mama!" Danilo stood directly in front of her, arms folded and looking irate. "You're supposed to pretend with your face when I'm talking for you. Play right!"

Isabel blinked. "Oh. I'm sorry, I was thinking."

Danilo rolled his eyes and moved where Mercedes—who stood behind Isabel holding her wrists—could read his lips.

"I think I'll take a shopping trip today," shrilled Danilo, mimicking his mother's voice, and Mercedes flapped Isabel's hands comically. "I don't have a *thing* to wear."

Isabel got into the game, batting her eyelids, and the other children giggled.

"What if somebody asks me out on a date?" Danilo said, and Mercedes patted Isabel's cheeks with her own hands.

"What?" exclaimed Isabel. She tried to stand up, but was hampered by Mercedes's arms on her shoulders.

"You're not allowed to talk, Mom," Danilo reminded her in his own voice, hands on hips. "You're supposed to look happy."

Isabel sat back down. She glanced at Benny, who was convulsed with laughter.

"I'm gonna kiss him!" was Danilo's next falsetto bombshell. "Kissy-kissy-kissy!" Isabel found herself in helpless giggles as she tried to pucker her lips, while Mercedes wrapped her arms in a ridiculous self-hug.

Suddenly she realized every eye in the room was trained on the door at the side of the room. All the children were shrieking in laughter, and Eli stood there hiding a smile.

"Oh!" Isabel gasped, unable to move.

Eli sauntered toward her, took her hands, and pulled her to her feet. "Kissy-kissy-kissy, Isabel," he murmured. "You're supposed to look happy."

"I—I—"

Eli turned to Danilo. "Is it okay if I borrow *la títere* for a few minutes?"

"Sure, why not," Danilo said magnanimously. "She's not very good at it anyway."

Isabel found herself led outside, where it was just beginning to get dark, a few stars sparkling overhead.

Eli sat on the porch step and tugged Isabel down beside him. "I'm sorry I haven't been over before now," he said, disarming some of her hurt. "I had something I wanted to take care of before I came."

"That's okay. I did wonder…" But she couldn't admit how self-centered she'd felt about his failure to call. She fell silent, suddenly shy. Now that he was here, she didn't know what to say.

She looked at his hand, which still held hers, and jumped a little when he kissed her knuckles. "How are things going here with Benny?"

Distracted, she looked at his mouth, which nuzzled her fingers. "Good. Fine. I like it." She wasn't sure what he'd asked her.

He grinned a little. "I'm glad, because I'm hoping she'll let you stay a little longer until we can find a place to live."

"A place to live?" His lips had moved to her palm, and she couldn't think of anything original to say. "Who?"

"You. Me. Danilo and Mercedes. We definitely need a yard."

"I don't need a yard. I'm moving to… Eli, would you stop that?"

"Okay." He released her wrist and took her face in his hands. "Kiss, Isabel."

She couldn't help it, he was right there and all she had to do was tilt her head a little.

"Man," he said after a minute, "I'm going to enjoy doing that for the rest of my life."

"You know," she swallowed, "I think there's something you forgot."

"Yeah." He shook his head ruefully. "I said I would wait until you came to me, but you *did* say you loved me. Even though I think you only did it because you thought you were going to die. Still…I'm pretty sure it counts."

Isabel started to laugh. "It counts. Eli, are you asking me to marry you?"

His eyes widened. "D-d-didn't I ask you?"

"Well, no," she said apologetically.

"Come on, Isabel, cut me some slack. I've never done this before."

"Done what?" she asked with false innocence.

Eli shook his head. "Okay, let me start over. I love you, Isabel, and I want to be your husband. I want to help you raise Danilo and Mercedes." The tenderness in his eyes had Isabel blinking away tears. "The reason it took me so long to get over here to ask, is because I've been trying to work out a transfer to San Antonio. I want you to be able to go to college, and I know how hard it is for you to live here where so many painful things have happened."

Isabel could hardly breathe. "Eli, you can't leave Border Patrol for me!"

"Well, I could," he said with a shrug, "but I won't have to. There's a Border Patrol job there, and Dean says I have a pretty good chance of getting it. Do you think—" He swallowed. "Do you think you could compromise just a little bit?"

Isabel felt hope banging around in her chest. "I don't know what to say." He had already done so much for her—

"I hope you'll say yes, because otherwise we're going into a custody battle over that big brown mutt in my Jeep."

Isabel jumped to her feet. "Mutt? What mutt?"

"Fonzie turned up in Mrs. Peterson's backyard yesterday, going through her trash." Eli stood up and followed Isabel, who was running toward his vehicle.

Sure enough there was Fonzie, nose hanging over the open side, tongue lolling. She grabbed the dog in a hug.

"The children will be so excited!"

"Okay, so was that a 'yes' on the yard?" he asked, rubbing a hand around the back of his neck.

Isabel whirled to throw her arms around Eli. "That's a 'yes' on everything!"

Staggering a bit, he laughed and kissed her hard. "Do you really love me, Isabel? Enough to be my wife in spite of my job?"

"Beyond what I could ever have imagined," she

breathed, kissing his cheek. "Eli, your job is part of who you are, and I'd never be so presumptuous as to throw that away. Hasn't God been good, to help us find one another?"

"Oh, yeah," he said with deep satisfaction in his voice. After another long kiss he suddenly raised his head. "I told you I was bad at this stuff."

Isabel had trouble uncrossing her eyes. "I think you're catching on pretty fast."

Eli grinned. "No, I meant I forgot something else." He leaned inside the Jeep, muttering an impatient "Back off, Fonzie," as he reached into the glove box. "Here it is." He opened his hand to reveal a black velvet box nestled in his palm.

"Oh, my." Isabel took the box and opened it with shaking fingers. Inside was a turquoise ring, set in twists of silver with small diamonds on either side—a design utterly unlike the gold solitaire set she'd lost in the fire, but just as beautiful. She looked up at the man who was to be her husband, immersing herself in the love in his eyes. "Will you put it on my finger?" she whispered.

"Okay." He awkwardly took the ring out of the box, which he tucked into his pocket, then picked up her hand. "I picked it out, but my mom said you'd like it."

Isabel stood quietly, tears trembling on the ends of her lashes, as Eli slid the dainty ring onto her engagement finger. "I love you, Eli Carmichael, and you'd better get used to hearing it." She laced her fingers through his and stepped close to him, looking straight up into his blue eyes. "I'm going to spend the rest of my life learning to be the companion and friend and lover you deserve."

Eli touched his lips to the turquoise ring, then kissed her lips again. "Okay, then we'll be in class together. I love you, Isabel."

Look for the next exciting book in
THE TEXAS GATEKEEPERS *series,*
coming in April 2006.
Owen Carmichael and Bernadette Malone
are on the run from a killer in
ON WINGS OF DELIVERANCE,
only from Elizabeth White
and Love Inspired Suspense!

Dear Reader,

Last year I eagerly accepted a spot in the van during my church's annual trek to south Texas. I knew I was going to set my next book there and could simultaneously research and "do ministry." I didn't know it was going to change my heart.

The poverty, heat and dust were no surprise. But I also found warm hearts, bright smiles and the universal language of kinship in Christ. I discovered how richly blessed we are in the U.S. and that sharing my faith brings unspeakable joy.

Visiting Mexico prepared me to write *Sounds of Silence,* as I tried to put myself inside the skin of people not like me. How would it feel to be a traumatized, hearing-impaired orphan? What would it be like to violently lose your husband and then fall in love with a man in his same profession? Going to Mexico helped me to see that all of us experience seasons of deep need and loneliness—and that those in Christ have something to share, whether you're a Spanish-speaking child or a Texas construction worker or an Alabama housewife.

Much of this story is filled with the starkness of the Mexican hills and border slums. But often in the greatest deprivation, God reveals Himself to be our true and faithful refuge. I encourage you to go to His Word, the Bible, to find strength and encouragement. If you have questions or if you have something to share with me, I would love to hear from you via my Web site, www.elizabethwhite.net. Or you may write to me at Steeple Hill Books, 233 Broadway, Suite 1001, New York, NY 10279.

In the meantime, I hope you enjoy the story! Stay tuned for *On Wings of Deliverance,* the third book in the Texas Gatekeepers series.

Blessings,

Elizabeth White

Love Inspired
SUSPENSE
RIVETING INSPIRATIONAL ROMANCE

A Time To Protect

by Lois Richer

Nurse Chloe Tanner stopped a would-be assassin from killing the mayor of Colorado Springs, and it is FBI agent Brendan Montgomery's job to protect the single mom. No one said anything about protecting his own heart....

Faith at the Crossroads: Can faith and love sustain two families against a diabolical enemy?

Don't miss this first book in the Faith at the Crossroads series.

On sale January 2006

Available at your favorite retail outlet.

Steeple Hill®

REQUEST YOUR FREE BOOKS!

2 FREE INSPIRATIONAL NOVELS
PLUS A
FREE
MYSTERY GIFT

Love Inspired®

YES! Please send me 2 FREE Love Inspired® novels and my FREE mystery gift. After receiving them, if I don't wish to receive any more books, I can return the shipping statement marked "cancel." If I don't cancel, I will receive 4 brand-new novels every month and be billed just $3.99 per book in the U.S., or $4.74 per book in Canada, plus 25¢ shipping and handling per book and applicable taxes, if any*. That's a savings of over 20% off the cover price! I understand that accepting the 2 free books and gift places me under no obligation to buy anything. I can always return a shipment and cancel at any time. Even if I never buy another book from Steeple Hill, the two free books and gift are mine to keep forever.

113 IDN D74R 313 IDN D743

Name	(PLEASE PRINT)	
Address		Apt.
City	State/Prov.	Zip/Postal Code

Signature (if under 18, a parent or guardian must sign)

Order online at www.LoveInspiredBooks.com

Or mail to Steeple Hill Reader Service™:

IN U.S.A.	IN CANADA
3010 Walden Ave.	P.O. Box 609
P.O. Box 1867	Fort Erie, Ontario
Buffalo, NY 14240-1867	L2A 5X3

Not valid to current Love Inspired subscribers.

Want to try two free books from another series?
Call 1-800-873-8635 or visit www.morefreebooks.com

* Terms and prices subject to change without notice. NY residents add applicable sales tax. Canadian residents will be charged applicable provincial taxes and GST. This offer is limited to one order per household. All orders subject to approval. Credit or debit balances in a customer's account(s) may be offset by any other outstanding balance owed by or to the customer.

LIREG05

Love Inspired
SUSPENSE

TITLES AVAILABLE NEXT MONTH

Don't miss these two stories in January

A TIME TO PROTECT by Lois Richer
Faith at the Crossroads

When Chloe Tanner witnesses an attempt on Mayor
Maxwell Vance's life, she becomes the next target. Agent
Brendan Montgomery is assigned to find the mayor's
would-be assassin and keep Chloe alive. He's drawn to
the single mother, but with a dangerous man on the loose,
he can't afford to be distracted.

EVEN IN THE DARKNESS by Shirlee McCoy
A LAKEVIEW novel

Tori Riley would do anything to keep the daughter she gave
up for adoption safe from the men who were after her—even
depend on former DEA agent Noah Stone. He didn't trust
Tori's motives, but there was no time for questions, for
every second brought an unscrupulous enemy closer to
Tori's daughter....

LISCNM1205